A Head Over Heels Christmas

To Carol,

A Head Over Heels Christmas

with love,

Sara Downing

Sara Downing
x

For Mum
1942-2019

The Four Families

The Brookes Family

Evie and James

And their two daughters:

Imogen (21) and Anastasia (19)

Plus Pascal, Imogen's boyfriend

The Hopper Family

Alex and Mark

And their five children:

Archie (19), Millie (17), Rosie (14),
Bertie (10) and Lucie (4)

The Parry Family

Grace & Tom

And their ten year old twins, Lily
& Jack

The Tizzaro Family

Lydia (Evie's sister) and Vincenzo

And their two children, Emilia (4)
and Francesco (2)

Chapter One – The Brookes Family

Evie gazed down at the patchwork quilt of emerald hills, terracotta roofs and azure pools. The low winter sun cast disproportionately long shadows from the slender cypresses which stood sentry along winding roads to secluded villas.

She sighed with contentment and delved into her handbag for her phone, but was spotted by a passing air hostess: 'I'm afraid you need to put your bag under your seat now please, madam, ready for landing.'

Evie tucked her phone between her knees and duly dropped her bag to the floor. The captain had announced earlier that those on the left side of the plane would have a great view of the Duomo and she wanted to get a good shot. Although she had visited many times before, she was always fascinated to see such iconic buildings, so commanding from the ground, looking like they were part of a model village. She glanced across at Anastasia and James to make sure they had fastened their seat belts.

As the hills and villas gave way to factory outlets and industrial estates the plane banked sharply. Evie gulped.

'S'OK, Mum,' said Anastasia, putting a hand over her

mother's. 'I'll look after you.'

At nineteen, and in the midst of a gap year, Ana now considered herself the most well-travelled of the family. Evie had to concede that she probably would be by the time the year was up, however as a seasoned traveller herself she wasn't ready for this sudden role reversal. She didn't consider that she needed looking after by the younger generation just yet.

'I'm not scared,' Evie said. 'Just excited.'

'This is gonna be great,' said Ana. 'It's gonna be so good to catch up with the others. Feel like I haven't seen them in ages. What time does Immy's plane get in?'

'Just before ours, all being well. Not too long to wait to see big sis,' said Evie. She and James hadn't seen their eldest daughter, Imogen, since the end of the summer either, and Evie was equally impatient. In her fourth and final year at Exeter, Immy had gone straight to Paris when the Christmas break had begun, to be with her French boyfriend, Pascal. They had met a few summers earlier, during a family holiday in the Dordogne. Evie had thought – hoped, even – that the intense romance which had sparkled poolside would have fizzled out with the return to English drizzle, but it hadn't. Then when Immy scored A*s in French at both GCSE and A Level, and decided to study the language at university as well, Evie had a feeling that Pascal was going to be a part of Immy's life for the foreseeable future. When Immy had stipulated in her year abroad application that she wished to be in or near to Paris, Evie had to accept the fact that the relationship was serious. Immy had been successful in her request, with a posting to a small town not far from Versailles, and whilst she spent her weekdays as an *assistante anglaise* at a French high school, and every weekend with Pascal in the fashionable Sixth Arrondissement, their feelings for one another had only grown stronger. It wasn't that Evie didn't like Pascal – she really did, and he was perfectly charming – she just didn't want Immy bound by the constraints of a serious relationship too young.

'I have someone to practise *la langue francaise* on now, *ma chere maman*,' Immy had said to her mother, 'whenever I want. Anything less than a First for my oral paper will be a massive disappointment.' Evie knew enough French to understand that the same word – *langue* – was employed to mean both language and tongue. She didn't like to dwell on it; her daughter was an adult now, and Evie couldn't be responsible for what she got up to. All she could do was hope she was being careful.

'Look, there it is,' yelled Ana, leaning over her mother from the middle seat. 'It looks so little.'

'Did you get a good shot?' asked James, bashing his Financial Times along its centre and folding it into his lap.

'Yeah, look,' said Ana, grabbing her mother's phone and thrusting it under her father's nose.

'Hey, not so quick,' said Evie, snatching it back. There were no secrets on her phone, none whatsoever, but she suffered the same blind panic as her offspring if forcibly removed from it for more than a few seconds.

'Is Auntie Lydia picking us up?' said Ana.

Evie's younger sister had lived in Florence since

spending the third year of her own degree in the city. With husband Vincenzo Tizzaro, once her university tutor, and their two young children, she lived in a small but beautiful villa in the hills around Florence. Evie and James were frequent visitors. Sometimes they stayed with Evie and Vincenzo, but this time they had booked into a hotel.

'It's too much to expect you to put us all up for Christmas,' Evie had said. 'There are too many of us this time.'

'We can still eat out on the big day,' Lydia said. 'But I'd love to have you all here. Really I would.'

Evie didn't want to have to spell it out to her sister that the thought of sharing the single – yet huge – guest bathroom at the villa with a multitude of family members didn't hold any appeal for her. She liked her creature comforts too much, as did James. 'Anyway, I've booked Christmas lunch for us all at the Four Seasons, then it's no trouble for anyone,' said Evie.

'Then at least let me have the girls to stay here,' said Lydia. 'I don't see so much of them these days. Pascal is very welcome, too, of course.'

Evie wished she could have Immy on the trip without Pascal. Just like the old days, when the girls were younger. Sometimes it was hard to accept that her daughters had grown up and were moving on.

Immy and Ana hadn't been to Florence since early 2016, when they had flown out as a family to visit Lydia's new-born daughter, Emilia. Evie still saw plenty of her sister; Lydia frequently took the children back to the UK to visit her parents, and Evie needed no excuse to pop over to Florence when she could, but they were long past the days of dragging the girls along on every trip they made. Since Lydia and Vincenzo's latest little darling, Francesco, now aged two, had arrived, Evie found it hard to resist the call of cuteness, especially as empty-nest syndrome was a frequent visitor to the Brookes' household. Sometimes one adorable photo on Facebook of his latest milestone was all it took to trigger another flight booking.

'Where did you say we'd meet them?' said James, as they followed the trail of passengers through to the arrivals zone.

'There's Pascal over there,' shouted Ana, pointing, and almost leaving the floor with excitement. 'By the baggage carousel.' She ran across the hall and threw herself into his arms.

'Ana, it is very lovely to see you,' said Pascal, kissing Ana on both cheeks – twice over – before holding her at arm's length and studying her. 'You are very brown. Suits you, *ma cherie*. Very beautiful, *comme ta soeur*.'

Ana blushed. She thought her sister's boyfriend got better looking every time she set eyes on him. Sometimes she couldn't help but wonder what would have happened if she had pursued the relationship with Julien, the French boy that she had met on the same holiday. It was a shame they'd just been too young, as that drawling French accent made her insides melt. 'Where's Immy?'

'Oh, she needed the toilet, she's coming back very soon.'

'There she is, there she is,' shouted Ana, spotting her sister's dark head over the crowds. 'Over here, Mum.' Ana went to run towards her sister, but as the crowds parted between them, she screeched to a halt. They all saw it at the same time. It was impossible not to see.

'Holy shit,' said James.

'You are joking me,' said Ana. 'Jeez, Immy, what have you done?'

'I think that's perfectly obvious, don't you?' said James, glaring at Pascal.

'Mum, Dad, Ana, you wouldn't believe how much I've missed you all,' said Immy, reaching to hug each of her family members in turn. 'Merry Christmas! We're going to have the best holiday ever.'

Chapter Two – The Parry Family

Tom had spotted the sign for the shuttle bus to the car hire terminal.

'C'mon, kids, this way,' he said to their ten-year-old twins. 'Hold my hand, Lily. Jack, you go with Mummy.'

'Why do we have to hire a car, Daddy?' asked Lily, as they wheeled their suitcases behind them. 'Auntie Evie's got a big posh limo to take them to their hotel.'

'Well, we thought it might be useful to have a car, in case we want to get out of Florence and go exploring. We're here for longer than the others, remember. They all go home the day after Boxing Day, but Mummy and Daddy have more time off than they do, so we thought it would be nice to stay. There are some lovely villages to explore round here.'

'Oh,' said Lily. 'Does that mean we have to go in churches and museums?'

'Maybe some, but there'll be some nice shops, too, I'm sure.' Lily's eyes widened.

The spring term didn't start till early January, although as head teacher and deputy head of two separate schools, Tom and Grace had to go back a couple of days before term started officially. Either way they still had time on their hands, and as they hadn't been to Florence before, they wanted to make the most of the trip. Grace had listened to Evie raving about the city so many times, she wanted to experience it for herself.

'Daddy,' Lily began, in the lilting voice she used when a big question was brewing. Tom could practically see the cogs turning in her mind.

'Yes, Lily,' said Tom as they reached the bus stop.

'Do Italian people eat the same food as us?'

'Of course they do,' said Tom. 'We eat Italian food at home all the time, don't we?'

'Like pasta and stuff?'

'Lily, you know exactly what Italian people eat. You love pasta and pizza and mozzarella, and all those kind of things, don't you?'

'I know I do,' said Lily. 'And tiramisu. But at home they're just in the shops. We have to buy them. Here, they must grow them, because *that's* where they come from. They must have to grow the pasta and the pizzas here, and then they send them to England, to sell in the shops.'

'Oh Lily, you are a silly sausage sometimes,' said Tom. 'You know that pasta doesn't grow. Nor pizzas. Don't you remember when we went on that pasta making course for Mummy's birthday?'

Lily laughed, bending double. 'Oh, Daddy, you're the silly one,' said Lily, prodding her father in the stomach, 'because you couldn't tell I was winding you up, could you? Mummy says I'm really good at winding Jack up, so I thought I'd try it out on you.'

'Oh, that's so nice of you, thank you,' said Tom, wondering at how his daughter's mind worked sometimes. 'You're such a monkey. Look, here we go.'

The shuttle bus pulled up and they hauled their bags up the steps. Jack ran straight to the back and sat down.

Grace spotted an elderly man in need of a seat. 'Jump up, Jack,' she said. 'Let the man sit down please.'

'*Grazie signora*,' said the man, settling down with a groan. '*Ciao bello, bella*,' he said, smiling at the twins, who turned their biggest and most charming smiles on him.

'How old?' he said, switching to English.

'They're ten,' said Grace.

'Ah, *i gemelli*,' said the man. '*Che divertimento.*'

'Mummy,' said Jack.

'Just a minute, love, I'm talking.'

'But Mummy.'

There was a loud squelch and the air around Jack turned fetid.

'Jack just chuffed,' said Lily, disapproval written on her face.

'That's what I was trying to tell you,' said Jack, frowning at his mother.

The pair of them looked at the man, whose face crinkled into laughter lines.

'I'm so sorry,' said Grace.

'Ah, *l'innocenza della giovinezza*, the innocence of youth,' he said, waving his hand in the air, in true Italian style. '*I belli gemelli.*'

'They're not so beautiful when they do that,' laughed

9

Grace.

When they pulled up at the car hire terminal, Tom helped the man unload his luggage onto the pavement.

'*Mille grazie*,' he said. 'I come here for Christmas from Sicily. I visit my daughter and my granddaughter. She ten, too. I have much laughs, I think.' He patted the twins fondly on their heads.

'Well, I hope you all have a very merry Christmas, signor,' said Grace. 'Come on you two monsters, let's go and get our car, before you cause any more trouble.'

The Europcar queue was by far the longest. Grace and Tom parked the twins on a nearby bench with a packet of crisps each and strict instructions not to move.

'At this rate we'll miss Christmas day,' said Tom. Neither could grasp the strange queuing system which seemed to favour those who had booked directly with the company, and not through a comparison site, like they had.

Grace noticed a pair of middle-aged women in the next line along nudging each other and staring at Tom. 'Don't look now, but I think you've got a couple of admirers over there,' she said.

But Tom swung straight round, immediately catching the eye of one of the women, who collapsed into fits of giggles.

'It's him, I'm sure of it,' she said to her friend, in a strong Geordie accent.

'Go on then, see if you can get a selfie. Ask him, Shirl, you've nothing to lose.'

'Watch out, they're coming over,' said Grace.

'Excuse me, but aren't you that bloke off the telly?' said the woman, flicking her hair over her shoulder, and batting her (unnaturally long, Grace thought) eyelashes.

'No, I'm sorry, you're mistaken,' said Tom, giving the women a dazzling smile nonetheless. 'I've never been on TV in my life.'

'C'mon, don't be shy,' said the other woman. 'We loved your latest film, didn't we, Shirl. You were the detective, the one with the nice hair.'

'Well, it's very flattering, but I'm really not him, whoever he is. I might have a double out there somewhere, but I'm so sorry to disappoint you.'

They didn't look like they believed him, but fortunately for Tom, the women were called forward for their turn. 'Well, you can see how he'd be a bit shy, when he's with his family and all,' said the other one, with a backwards glance at him. 'He's just being modest. He's a bit taller than he looks on the telly, though, isn't he?'

'They didn't believe me, did they?' said Tom. 'Who the hell do they think I am?'

'God knows,' said Grace. 'I can't think of anyone on TV who looks like you.'

Lily and Jack came bounding over. 'Who were those ladies, Daddy?'

'Oh, they thought Daddy was someone famous,' said Grace.

'Ha, that's hilarious,' said Jack. 'Don't they know Daddy's not a celeb, he's just a headmaster. Everyone in our school knows who he is, but that's it.'

11

'Well, thank you for putting us right on that, Jack,' said Tom, laughing.

'It's over here, Daddy,' yelled Lily. In a sea of Fiat 500's, they had finally found theirs.

'Oh, this is cute,' said Grace, leaping into the driver's seat. 'I've always fancied driving one of these.'

'I'll load up then, shall I?' said Tom, rolling his eyes as he surveyed the pile of bags that his family had dumped at the rear. 'Good job we only brought small bags. Kids, you'll have to have your backpacks on your laps.'

'Look, Daddy, there's that lady again,' Lily yelled through the hatchback.

The two women who had pounced on Tom were circling a shiny red Alpha Romeo convertible, parked a few spaces down from theirs. They looked up and caught his eye. 'Nice car,' said Tom.

'I have to spend the divorce settlement on something,' said the woman who wasn't Shirley. 'Can't take it with you, can you?'

'Well, enjoy it,' said Tom, closing the boot of the Fiat and climbing into the passenger seat.

'Maybe they'll believe you're not rich and famous, now they've seen what we're driving compared to that flash thing,' said Grace.

Tom laughed and looked over his shoulder at the children. 'Everyone ready for our Italian adventure?' he said. '*Andiamo!*'

'Ooh, everything's the wrong way round,' said Grace, lurching out of the parking space and stalling the car.

Chapter Three – The Hopper Family

'And here are your key cards, sir,' said the immaculately dressed man on reception. 'One king room with an extra bed and two twins. They are all on the same corridor. We will bring your bags to your rooms shortly. I hope you will have a very pleasant stay at the Savoy.'

'Thank you, I'm sure we will,' said Mark.

The receptionist beckoned to a bellboy and indicated the enormous pile of bags surrounding the Hopper family. The bellboy tried to hide his horrified expression as he began loading up his trolley.

'I'm so sorry,' said Mark's wife, Alex, to the bellboy. 'It's really hard trying to travel light with five kids.'

'Four, actually,' said Mark. 'But hey. Still a lot of stuff.' Their eldest – Mark's stepson, Archie – would be arriving separately. Having deferred his marine biology degree by a year, he was currently based in Méribel, working as a chalet host for the ski season. Fortunately he had managed to secure a few days' leave and his train was due in that afternoon.

'Following in your father's footsteps, aren't you?' Alex had said to him, when he secured the job. She'd cupped his face with her hands and kissed him on the forehead. 'He would have been so proud of you.' Alex's first husband, Peter, had died of a brain tumour when Archie was almost six. Archie had always borne a strong resemblance to Peter, and now, as a young adult, he resembled so uncannily the young man that Alex had married, that sometimes her heart turned somersaults when she looked at him.

Peter had been a celebrated travel writer with many books to his name; they still sold well, even fourteen years after his death. His first book had been a guide to the ski season for gap year students, and now Alex saw Archie's choice of destination as the ultimate tribute he could pay his father.

'Wow, is this all for me?' shouted ten-year-old Bertie, flinging open the door to his room.

'No, you know full well it isn't,' said Mark, smiling indulgently at his son. Bertie ran in and threw his backpack onto one of the beds.

'Do I really have to share with Archie?'

'Of course you do. Anyway, you're looking forward to seeing him as much as we are, aren't you?' said Mark.

'Yeah, I know. Just that this place is…' He ran into the bathroom. 'Wow, Daddy, it's amazing! Come and see the bath – it's huge!'

As well as being a stepfather to Archie, Alex had two daughters, Millie and Rosie. Millie was too young to remember her real father, and Alex had been pregnant with Rosie when Peter died, and so for the girls Mark *was* their dad – there was nothing *step* about him in their eyes. Young Bertie had come along not long after Mark had moved in with Alex, and now there was four year old Lucie, too, who had been something of an unexpected surprise.

'We really need to get you done now, Mark,' Alex had joked, on finding out that she was expecting her fifth child. 'Five really is enough, isn't it? How will we ever get to go on holiday with five children?'

But Mark wasn't so convinced that it was time to stop. He loved to see Alex surrounded by her brood and was immensely proud of them all, irrespective of their bloodline. Although he and Alex were well and truly on the wrong side of forty-five, and he knew their decision made sense, he couldn't help the pang of loss that he felt as Alex drove him to the hospital. He knew he should be thankful for the wonderful family they had already, and the fact that they were fortunate, between his salary as a lawyer and the royalties from Peter's books, to be able to give the children the kind of lifestyle they wanted for them. It was a luxury not many large families had.

'Bertie, can you choose a bed and unpack your stuff?' said Alex. 'And make sure you hang up your smart shirt for Christmas Day. Archie just messaged to say he'll be here in half an hour. Can we trust you to be sensible till then? We're only a couple of doors down. Be good, OK?'

They closed the door on Bertie and crossed their fingers, grimacing. They both knew their youngest son never did anything the easy way.

The two eldest girls were sharing a room opposite the

boys'. Alex knocked on their door and Rosie opened it.

'All OK, girls?'

'Millie's sulking,' said Rosie.

'What's up Mills?' said Alex. Her eldest daughter removed an AirPod from one ear with such force that Mark was surprised her earlobe didn't come with it.

'Do I have to share with *her*?' she said, jabbing a thumb in her sister's direction.

'You do.'

'Why can't I have my own room? She's a kid.'

'Technically so are you, Millie,' said Mark. 'For a few months more, at least. Anyway just look at this room. It's bigger than some people's apartments. Really, sweetheart, you should be more grateful. And try to be nice, eh? It is Christmas and this is only for four nights and I'm sure you two can manage not to kill each other for that long. And your sister isn't a baby. She's fourteen, and you were fourteen not that long ago, remember? The other option would be sharing with Archie, and I can't see that working out too well.'

'At least he's more interesting,' said Millie. 'And an adult.'

'Hey, thanks, sis,' said Rosie. 'Really.'

'Just think about his room at home,' said Alex. 'I'm not sure you'd cope with his dirty pants on the bathroom floor.'

'Humphh,' said Millie, jabbing her AirPod back in and picking up her phone with an eye-roll.

'Anyway, we'll leave you to unpack, shall we?' said Alex, raising one eyebrow.

'Teenagers,' sighed Mark as they closed the door.

'Yeah, and of those we have plenty,' said Alex. 'With more still to come. Can you imagine what Bertie will be like, once the hormones take hold?'

They pushed open the door to their own room, which they were sharing with Lucie. Their four year old daughter hadn't moved. She lay, starfish-like and snoring, across their king-size bed, exhausted from the journey.

'Let's book a weekend away for just us two, next year,' said Mark, putting an arm over his wife's shoulders.

'Yeah, how about January?' said Alex, laughing.

As he tapped his key card on the sensor, Archie could hear singing and splashing.

'Hey, Bertie, I'm here,' he yelled, slamming the door to announce his presence.

'Dance for me, dance for me, dance for me, oh, oh, oh, I've never seen anybody do the things you do before.

They say move for me, move for me, move for me ay, ay, ay…'
Archie couldn't help laughing to himself.

'Bertie!' he called again, tapping on the bathroom door.

The singing stopped. 'That you, bro? Come in my G.'

'You decent?'

'You can't see my penis, if that's what you're asking.'

Archie laughed out loud this time. He had missed all of his siblings during his travels, but particularly his little brother. Despite the nine years between them, Bertie never failed to make him laugh, and had eased him through many moments of teenage angst, just by being himself.

He pushed open the bathroom door. Bertie lay in the enormous free-standing bath, bubbles up around his ears. The tap was still running and water was starting to lap over the edge.

'Hey mate, enough water don't you think?' said Archie, leaning over to turn off the tap.

'Waddya think of the bubbles then? I used the whole pot,' said Bertie, standing up. 'Oops, forgot I haven't got any clothes on.' He sat back down again, causing a tsunami of water and bubbles to cascade onto the floor.

'Oh shit,' said Archie, surveying the drenched bathroom floor. 'Pull the plug out now, before you start a flood, eh?'

'It's cool,' said Bertie, jumping out of the bath and grabbing a fluffy robe from a hook. It came down to his ankles. Bertie flipped up the hood.

'You look like some sort of weird bubbly monk,' said Archie, as he began to mop the floor with towels. His little brother was a pickle, but more often than not it was impossible to be angry with him; Bertie just couldn't help himself. 'Let's get this lot cleaned up before Mum and Dad see it, shall we?'

'Need to give you a hug first, my bro,' said Bertie, lunging at his brother. 'Missed you.' The long robe caught under his foot and he lurched backwards, his bottom sliding along the wet floor. He careered towards his brother, feet first, taking Archie down with him. The pair of them lay amidst the water and bubbles, laughing their hearts out.

'Oh Bertie, whatever will you do next?' said Archie, grabbing his brother and pulling him into a hug.

'Give me a minute, I'll think of something,' said Bertie.

'Well, before you do, let's give housekeeping a call and get them to bring us some more towels. And I need to get these jeans off. They're soaked.'

'Promise you won't tell Mum and Dad?'

'Course I won't. Anyway, you're clean. They'll be happy that you've had a proper wash for once.'

'Hey, you saying I smell?'

'Wouldn't dare.'

Chapter Four – The Brookes Family

The sleek black Mercedes pulled up outside the Four Seasons Hotel. A swarm of immaculate black suits appeared from nowhere. Two of the suits executed some impressively synchronised door opening, another reached into the boot for their luggage and – did that one really just bow? No, Evie must have imagined it.

She and James had spent the short drive from the airport in near silence, eyes fixed but unseeing on the city's familiar architecture. Once or twice Evie had caught the chauffeur looking at them in his mirror, probably wondering just how harmonious their luxury stay was going to be, considering they were barely on speaking terms. But it wasn't that. Each was too shocked at what they had seen; neither had processed this new piece of information and therefore neither knew what to say to the other.

'Signore, signora Brookes, welcome back to the Four Seasons, Florence. We are delighted to have you stay with us again.' A tall, slim man, who introduced himself as Alberto Marcelli, the Front Desk Manager, shook their hands and beckoned for them to follow him into the foyer.

Evie loved this place. She and James had stayed a handful of times and each visit had been utterly perfect. There was no hotel in the world, she thought, that spoilt its guests quite as much as this place did. Nothing was too much trouble. 'It's never too much trouble if you pay people enough,' James would say. Even if that was the case, Evie thought it was worth it.

'Can we retire here one day?' she had joked with James once, as they lay sprawled on the huge bed in their executive suite, exhausted after a day of shopping and sightseeing. 'We could sell the house, run away to Florence, and live here till all our money ran out. The girls won't mind if we spend all their inheritance, will they?'

'Unless you're planning a very short retirement, I think the money would soon run out. At the rate you spend it round those shops, anyway. It is very special, though, isn't it.'

Today, though, their arrival had lost its usual gloss, but not through any fault of the hotel's. Shell-shocked, Evie stood in the foyer, gazing through to the beautiful loggia with its glass ceiling, marbled frescoes, statues and huge displays of fresh flowers on all surfaces. This time, the centre was graced with an enormous Christmas tree, bedecked in silver and white. On close inspection she saw that each tiny decoration was a glass angel. The whole place was a dream, and normally she would be in paroxysms of delight by now.

'Thank you for checking in online this morning, signore Brookes,' said Alberto. Evie had almost forgotten he was still with them. 'Our luggage team will bring your bags to your room momentarily, and I personally will take you there now.'

Only someone who had learnt English as a foreign language would use words like *momentarily*, Evie thought. She and James followed Alberto through the sumptuous corridors, their feet sinking into the deep pile carpet.

'Buona sera, signore e signora Brookes,' said a passing waiter, nodding to them.

They know our names already, and we've only just arrived, thought Evie. Normally she would lap this up. Today she managed a pinched smile and a barely audible greeting.

Evie had only managed to hang up her special dress for Christmas Day before she flopped onto the sofa with a sigh.

'How could she do that to us?' she said. 'And more importantly, how could she do that to herself? What about her degree? Her future?'

'I know. I can't believe she's done this – or rather *he's* done it. I should have bloody killed him the first time I set eyes on him.' The memory of that first encounter loomed large in James' mind now. One afternoon on their Dordogne holiday the adults had returned from a trip into a nearby town to find that a stranger – the son of the chateau owner's gardener, so their daughter informed them – was performing tricks in their pool, no doubt in an attempt to impress, or seduce, Immy. James still bridled when he recalled the unmistakeable lust his then sixteen-year-old daughter had exhibited at the sight of this toned and tanned boy. Man. He was a man then and a man now. James knew that, but although his eldest had also been an adult for some years, he still wasn't ready for another man to take pride of place in her life.

'It takes two, James. It's not all him. Or her.'

They hadn't had a chance to talk to Immy at the airport – which now Evie thought was probably just as well. It wasn't the right time or place, and as she could see James' temper bubbling just below the surface, it would have been awful if one of them had said something in the heat of the moment which they later came to regret. Thankfully their driver had been waiting and they'd been whisked away, too stunned to think.

Evie's phone pinged with a message from Immy. 'Sorry for the surprise, Mum. Can we talk later? Drinks in the Piazza at 6? Just me and Ana to start with.'

Lydia had met the girls and Pascal from the airport and taken them back to her house. It had always been the plan that the four families would then reconvene for drinks in the evening, once everyone had settled into their various accommodations. But this advance party had more of the feel of a COBRA crisis management meeting than a festive get-together. Evie read Immy's message to James. 'What on earth do we say to her?'

'God knows,' said James, sighing. 'I mean, clearly getting rid of it isn't an option now, is it? I can't believe we didn't notice this when she was home.'

'She must have kept it well hidden, and I suspect she probably didn't start to show till after she'd gone back to uni. Oh, but James, it breaks my heart that she didn't feel she could tell us. What kind of parents must we be, if she was too scared to say anything? She's gone through all that on her own. If we'd known earlier then we could have done something about it. Helped her.'

'Maybe that's what she was afraid of. She didn't say anything because she knew what we'd say. She knew we wouldn't want her to keep it. But she's a determined young woman and clearly she's made her mind up what she wants to do. There's no going back now, is there?'

'No, there isn't. Oh God, what are we going to do?'

'Well, I still want to kill the little French git, but I know that wouldn't help Immy. She's going to need him now, more than ever. That slimy bastard has attached himself pretty damn permanently now, hasn't he?'

Evie was broken-hearted. She couldn't see a way through this. Not one that would work out for the best for everyone. Some Christmas it was going to be. She had so been looking forward to having their family and friends all together for a few uncomplicated days. It was meant to be a relaxing break, eating, drinking and enjoying one another's company. Easy times and easy conversation. Now there was one topic that had jumped quite spectacularly to the top of the agenda and was bound to dominate the entire break.

'Let's go and have a drink in the bar first,' said James. He had been pacing up and down the room, running his fingers through his hair. 'We've got ages yet and I need a distraction. And a bit of Dutch courage.'

'Don't really feel like it,' said Evie. She flipped open the gift box that the hotel had left on the desk and picked up the card: 'The management would like to wish you a pleasant stay at the Four Seasons, Florence, and the compliments of the season.' She popped one of the champagne truffles into her mouth. 'Might just sit here and eat this lot instead.'

'No you won't,' said James, placing his hands on her shoulders. 'Come on, please? For me? This is our holiday, too, and we can't spend the whole time moping in our room, despite this massive shock. Freshen up and we'll go downstairs. We'll have a good chat with Immy later, sort things out, then hopefully we'll be able to relax a little. Everything will be alright.'

Evie didn't know how James could say that. How could he morph so quickly from premeditated murder to promises of hope? It had to be an act for her benefit. If anyone had ever asked her how she'd thought James would react to such shocking news, then anger would have been foremost in her mind for him. Below the surface it was obvious that he *was* angry; for some reason only known to him, he'd never really accepted Pascal into the bosom of the family. Evie thought this probably stemmed from the fact that Pascal was Immy's first serious boyfriend, and James, like many fathers before him, just wasn't ready to share her with another man yet. He would never admit to it, but no man was ever going to be good enough for his daughters, however hard they tried. And since the very moment they had first set eyes on Pascal, as James watched the younger man work his Gallic charm on mother and daughter alike, they'd had a competitive alpha male thing going on. Evie wasn't sure he would ever get over that.

She couldn't imagine how anything could ever be alright again. Their daughter's life was ruined, and all they could do was make the best of a bad situation. But Evie wasn't angry; instead she felt utterly bereft. All she could see was the precipice of a yawning great chasm in her relationship with her eldest daughter. How could Immy not have told them, and what did that say about the strength of their mother and daughter bond? It broke her heart.

Despite the gloom hanging over her, Evie couldn't help but exclaim as she glanced up at the high ceiling of the Atrium Bar, which was festooned with thousands of tiny white lights. She loved how the Italians did Christmas so tastefully and there was none of the British overdoing of decorations to the verge of tackiness. She would put money on it that these adornments had only gone up in early December, on the Feast of the Immaculate Conception, as was the tradition, and not in October, like they did at home. Another huge fir tree in the corner of this room was decorated with miniature glass baubles, which looked as though they were lit from within. The whole effect was mesmerising.

'Signore Brookes, welcome,' said the bartender, whose name tag read Ludo Sandri, Chief Mixologist. 'And your beautiful wife. Enchanted, signora. Welcome back to the Four Seasons. You like to see the cocktail menu or you have your usual? Atrium mojitos for you again this time?'

'Gosh, you have a very good memory,' said James. 'Are

they the ones with the raspberries?'

'Exactly, sir,' said Ludo.

'Then two of those, please,' said James.

'Please, do sit down, and I bring drinks to you,' said Ludo.

'They must keep notes,' James said to Evie, as they seated themselves on a velvet sofa on the far side of the bar. 'So that they can impress you when you come the next time.'

'Well it is impressive,' said Evie, managing to smile. 'Very impressive indeed. As always. I'd forgotten just how much I love it here.'

'You didn't forget, you're just a bit distracted,' said James, putting a hand over his wife's.

'So, how do we play it later?' said Evie. 'What on earth do we say to our twenty-one-year-old daughter, who's pregnant and about to sit her university finals? Talk about taking on too much at once.'

'I have absolutely no idea, sweetheart,' said James. 'But I'm hoping I'll find the words. Somehow or other.'

Evie and James made sure they arrived at the bistro in the piazza before the others. Evie always liked to be the first to arrive anywhere; somehow she always felt wrong-footed if she wasn't. Immy and Ana arrived shortly afterwards.

'Hello darlings,' said Evie, rising to kiss her daughters.

'Before the waiter comes over, Mum, Dad,' said Immy, pulling out a chair next to Evie, 'I know this must have come as a terrible shock, and I'm sorry I didn't say anything to you before, but what's done is done, and I hope that you will be able to find some happiness in your hearts for me. For both of us.'

'Jeez, Immy,' said Ana. 'Why can't you talk about this normally, like we did earlier with Auntie Lydia? Mum and Dad don't need to hear some weird speech you've been practising for hours.'

Evie and James hadn't known how their youngest daughter felt about Immy's news. The two of them had gone off with Lydia – and the perpetrator of the evil deed – from the airport, and they had only communicated via WhatsApp since. Ana hadn't said a lot, but then she never did in messages.

Evie wondered just how *normal* their discussion with Lydia had been. It twisted at her insides to know that her sister had been on hand to talk things through with Immy before she had. But their travel arrangements had been made a long time ago and everyone had been too shocked to react, so they had all gone off as intended, with plans to meet up that evening. In retrospect, a couple of hours apart before they met again had been a good thing. She and James had had time to calm down – even if only a little.

Evie was relieved that Pascal had the decency to remain behind while the family talked. They had half an hour to themselves before he would be joining them, along with Lydia and her family. Their friends would be along later, too. At the moment she wasn't sure how her husband would cope when Pascal did arrive. James wasn't a violent man, but in defence of his daughter's honour, who knew what he was capable of?

'How could you be so careless, Immy?' said Evie. She knew her tone of voice was too accusatory, but she couldn't help herself. 'I thought we'd brought you up to be more responsible than this. What about your degree? What about your life?'

'Mum, it'll be fine,' said Immy. 'Obviously we didn't set out to have a baby now. I mean, in an ideal world I'd be old, like thirty or something, before having kids, but it happened, and… well… we're so happy about it.'

'But have you thought about the practicalities of it all? How will you cope with finals with a baby? When's it due even?' said Evie.

'Twelfth of March.'

'Oh my God. Exams are in May. You'll barely be back on your feet by then. And what if you have to have a caesarean? How will you revise? You can't sit in the library with a baby crying all the time. You'll be stuck home feeding it, cleaning, washing, everything else. And that's before you even start on the sleepless nights.'

'OK, Mum,' said Immy. She turned to look at her mother and took a deep breath before speaking again. 'Was it really so awful when we came along? Were we really such a dreadful intrusion on your lives?'

Evie thought back to the early days of new motherhood. Her memory had wiped the bad stuff – rose-tinted spectacles were a perk of wisdom and maturity – and all she could think of was holding her perfect new baby close, and being unable to take her eyes from her little face and her rosebud lips. 'No,' she said softly. 'No, you weren't an intrusion at all. But for us it was the natural next step. We were older. Married. Had more money. Our futures were secure.' Now wasn't the time for Evie to remind Immy that actually she had fallen pregnant with her on their honeymoon, and they hadn't planned to start a family for a couple more years.

'We know all that. We've thought it through, really we have. And we've got plans. And don't worry Mum, none of it involves dumping the baby on you and leaving you to do all the work.'

Evie would never admit to the strength of the disappointment she had felt when she'd first set eyes on Immy at the airport. Aside from the impact on Immy's life, a grandchild for them now would mean some significant changes to their own transition period into a couple of empty-nesters. Evie's writing career was firmly established; her editor was expecting her to deliver the first draft of her latest novel in the spring. Where would playing nanny to her daughter and her new baby fit in with all that? And as for being a grandmother – a grandmother! Goodness, the label alone added twenty years, beige slacks and a walking stick to her, just like that. For her and James, the natural next step should be a few years of it being just the two of them, and the freedom to do all the things they hadn't been able to do when the girls were little and still living at home. But was she being selfish for thinking of the new life that she and James were carving out for themselves now? And her career? Should she instead be continuing to do what she had always done, which was to put her children first?

'Your mother didn't say that,' said James. 'We will help,

love, won't we?'

'Of course we will,' said Evie, unable to make eye contact with either of them.

'And what about me?' said Ana. 'No one has asked me what I think about all this?'

'Well, what *do* you think, darling?' said Evie, bracing herself.

'I think it's quite wonderful, actually,' said Ana, taking them all by surprise. She sat back and folded her arms. 'And Immy's so clever and so organised, she'll cope with it all. I can't wait to be an auntie.'

Evie and James stared at their younger daughter.

'I'm really glad you feel like that,' said Immy, pulling her sister close for a hug. 'Thank you. It's good to know you're on my side.'

Evie thought she saw an accusatory twinkle in both sets of daughters' eyes, but hoped it was just her imagination. She wondered how long Ana's joy at auntie-hood would last if both girls ended up back at home, post-uni and travels, with the addition of a baby who seemed to have taken over the house and who never slept.

'It has nothing to do with sides, and everything to do with making sure you're OK, Immy, and that you do what's best for you,' said James. 'For you. Not him.'

'Look, when Pascal's here, we'll talk you through our plans,' said Immy. 'But for now, don't worry, both of you. We're responsible adults. Pascal has a great job. He wants to look after us until I can get back to everything. We'll manage.' She patted her mother on the hand. 'We will, Mum, don't worry.'

The door to the bar swung open.

'Here they are,' said Evie.

The look on James' face when he rose to greet them said it all.

'Monsieur Brookes,' said Pascal. 'It is lovely to see you again. Madame Brookes'. He kissed Evie on the hand. Evie had told him many times to call them by their first names, but Pascal seemed to like the formality of Monsieur and Madame. James said he had no views on it either way, but Evie suspected he didn't want Pascal getting overly familiar.

James pulled himself up to his full height – which was about the same as Pascal's – and puffed out his chest. Evie wished he wouldn't posture like this. It was so unnecessary and as the older – and less fit – of the two, it did him no favours.

'Sit down, James,' she said to him, pulling him by the hand back into his seat. 'You look ridiculous.'

'Hello, properly, my lovely sister,' said Lydia, coming around the table to hug Evie. 'How are you?'

'I don't know, really,' said Evie.

'You'll be fine,' said Lydia. 'She's a sensible girl.'

'So where's Vincenzo?'

'He'll be along shortly with the children. He thought it might be a good idea to give you a few minutes with Pascal before he brought them in.'

'Thank you. Yes, James needs to lose his serial killer face before they arrive. Thank goodness you whipped them all away at the airport earlier, otherwise I dread to think what he'd have done to Pascal. You wouldn't think so to look at him now, but he was actually quite calm about the whole thing before we got here.'

'Oh really,' said Lydia. 'And you?'

'I'm heartbroken,' whispered Evie, trying not to brim up. Pascal beckoned to the bar tender as Immy shuffled up to make space for the new arrivals at the table. 'It kills me that she didn't tell me.'

'Yeah, I can imagine,' said Lydia. 'You'll sort this out, though. She loves you both so much, you know.'

'I know she does. But it's not what I wanted for her. Not yet. What about all that potential she has? She's so bright. I don't want it all to go to waste.'

'It won't. She'll still get there. Maybe just in a different order to you guys.'

'I wish I shared your optimism.'

'So, Pascal,' began James, his palms flat on the table. 'What have you got to say for yourself?'

'Dad!' said Immy. 'I'm not some pregnant teenager, out on the streets without a hope.'

'Let him speak, Immy,' said James. 'I want to hear what he's got to say. Besides which, you're not that far out of your teens, young lady.'

Immy scowled. Evie rolled her eyes. She knew it wouldn't do them any favours if James started to speak to Immy like she was a child again.

'Monsieur Brookes,' said Pascal, 'I love your daughter very much, and I want to spend my life with her. This baby – yes, it wasn't planned – but it will be the most cherished, most loved baby ever born, and Immy and he

33

or she will never be in want of nothing.'

'I hope you mean anything,' said James.

'Anything. Yes, my mistake. I'm very sorry. Immy will be so looked after. I relocate to England, you see. I am to come at the end of January.' Pascal worked for a large technology company based on the outskirts of Paris. James knew that they had offices around the world; he had checked the company out before Pascal started there.

'I have an excellent promotion, and because I speak good English, they are happy to relocate me to the UK. The new job will be in London, but at weekends I will be in Exeter with Immy. When the baby is born my parents will come to stay near her till Immy's exams are done. They have rented a property in Exeter already. Then after finals she will move to London to be with me permanently. It is all taken care of, Monsieur Brookes. You are not to worry about anything.'

'But where will you live?' said Evie. 'London's so expensive.'

'In London I will have an apartment provided by my company. It is very beautiful, I went to see it last week. In Kensington. We have big rooms and a park nearby for the pushing of the pram. Immy will love it. All the furniture, everything, it is all done. Even a cleaner.'

'Must be a big promotion, then,' said James, 'if they can send you to England, just like that.'

'It is,' said Immy.

'It sounds like you've thought it all through very well,' said Lydia.

'We planned it together,' said Immy, reaching for

Pascal's hand. 'And the timing of the relocation was an added bonus. We're so lucky it came at just the right time for us.'

When they had first met Pascal he had been helping out his father with maintenance at the chateau they were staying in. James had jumped to the immediate – and unjustified – conclusion that Pascal was some uneducated lout, dossing around over the summer and taking advantage of his situation to chat up as many visiting females as he could. Immy had allowed this to fester for a while, but when they'd returned home after the holiday she had revealed to her parents that Pascal had graduated in computer science earlier that summer. His speciality was artificial intelligence, and he was sitting on a couple of excellent job offers from prominent technology companies. In the five years since he had started work, he had risen sharply up the ranks.

'They love him there,' Immy said. 'He can do no wrong. He'll be the CEO in ten years, you wait.'

'That's very good to know,' said Evie. 'But this isn't just about the money, and the flat in London and all that goes with it. That all sounds great, but what about *your* career, Immy? What about the PGCE you wanted to do?'

'Mum,' said Immy, 'no one is forcing me to do anything I don't want to, here. We didn't *have* to have this baby. We *wanted* to.'

Immy had begun to consider teaching as a career in the early days of her degree. Her year in France as a language assistant in a school had then confirmed it for her.

'I'm still going to do it, but once the baby is a bit older

35

and can go to nursery. Once I can bear to part with him or her, Mum.'

Evie remembered that feeling. That deep sense that if you left your child with someone else for just one minute, you might miss something crucial and you'd never get that special moment back. 'I'm glad to hear it,' she said. 'I'm just worried about you not doing all the exciting things in your life you've always wanted to. I mean, you were going to travel after uni, too, weren't you?'

'I was. And we will. We can still travel with a baby in tow. It's not unheard of these days. And in any case, once it – and maybe its brother or sister – are all grown up, we'll still be young enough to see the world then, too. There's no rush to do everything now, is there?'

'I suppose,' said Evie.

'I'm happy about this, Mum, really I am. I don't feel like I'm throwing my life away. In fact I can't wait to meet this little one.' She rubbed her round stomach tenderly, and Pascal leaned over and kissed her on the cheek.

Evie and James exchanged a glance. Evie thought James looked less ready to kill than he had earlier, but it would be a while before either of them had their heads fully round this.

'So, what do you think about it all now?' Evie asked James as they strolled back to the hotel later. Evie clung tightly to her husband's arm; the alcohol had flowed freely all evening and she felt she had hit it too hard before the pizzas arrived to soak it up. She ought to sleep well tonight – if nightmares about her daughter's ruined life didn't keep her tossing and turning.

'I think she'll be OK,' said James. 'Despite everything I've always thought about him, which on the whole hasn't been good, he does seem committed, doesn't he? And they have a sensible plan of action.'

'They do. And she seems happy. I don't think she's doing this because she feels it's the only option available to her. I think she genuinely does want to do it. They seem to have such a perfect solution for everything, but I'm just terrified that it will all go horribly wrong at some point. It seems too perfect, somehow.'

'Don't think like that,' said James. 'Much as I still want to kill him just a little bit, I think they'll make a go of it. Well, they've got to, haven't they? And to give them their due, they both seem pretty mature about the whole thing.'

'I hate that his parents knew from the start, though. If they told them, why couldn't they have involved us in their plans?'

'Liberal French,' said James. 'It's all *laissez-faire* over there, isn't it?'

'A bit of a generalisation,' said Evie. 'And more than a tad racist, if I'm honest.'

'Yeah, but true,' said James. 'They probably are more accepting than us. We're a bit conventional, I suppose. But even so, I wish she'd felt she could say something.'

'We both know our daughter will only ever do what she wants to do, don't we?' said Evie. 'She won't be told. But it hurts, really it does.'

'I know,' said James, rubbing her shoulder. 'I think the others were a bit shocked, weren't they. Did you see their faces?'

The Parrys and the Hoppers had arrived together, and Vincenzo and the two children shortly afterwards. Vincenzo obviously knew about Immy's predicament, as he had seen the girls and Pascal earlier that afternoon, but in the midst of the reunions, the kissing of cheeks, the ordering of drinks, and the general mayhem of eleven young adults, teenagers and children reuniting for the first time in a while, Immy's bump had slipped under the radar to begin with. She had remained in her seat until the initial excitement died down and it wasn't until she stood up to go to the toilet that her secret was revealed.

'Oh my God,' said Archie. 'Immy's having a baby.'

Everyone had fallen silent. The adults had looked at Evie and James for a reaction, the teenagers' mouths had fallen open, and little Lucie, ever the one to state the obvious, had said: 'Immy's tummy's like a big fat balloon!'

When Immy replied: 'Yes, Lucie, it's huge!' the laughter that followed had broken the awkward silence. She knew it fell upon her to say something. 'Yes, folks, we do have a little piece of news. And no, you didn't know sooner, because nor did Mum and Dad and Ana. And we're sorry about that now, but it was our decision at the time not to say anything until we saw them.'

And then the questions had flown around thick and fast. When was it due, was she finishing her degree, where would they live, were they going to get married and if so, please could she be a bridesmaid? (Lucie again).

Evie was amazed that, once Ana knew, she hadn't messaged any of the others and tipped them off. She was actually relieved that it had stayed a secret until now, and they'd had a chance to discuss it as a family first.

Grace looked across at Evie and caught her eye. Her poor friend, she thought. What a shock.

'But we're really happy about it,' said Pascal. 'And we have lots of plans which we've just told Monsieur and Madame Brookes about. I think they will be happy for us, once they get over the shock.'

'It was a shock,' said James. He had to choose his words carefully, now that the audience was wider and contained young children. 'No doubt about it. But we're a family. We'll get through this.' As he took a swig of his beer, the smile he gave them didn't quite reach his eyes.

'Clearly he loves her,' James said now. 'And they're excited about the baby. I just hope their relationship is strong enough to survive this. They're so young.'

'They are young, but our daughter is a very determined woman,' said Evie.

'Yes, and I know where she gets that from,' said James. 'Still want to string him up and chop off his balls, though. That would be my preferred option.'

'Don't be daft, grandpa,' said Evie, wobbling on her high heels.

James laughed. 'Oh my God. We're going to be grandparents. We're too young, aren't we?'

'Yep, I thought so, but hey,' said Evie.

'So what will be your grandmother tag, then?' said James. 'Gran, granny, grandma, nanny, nana, grand-mama?'

'Oh blimey,' said Evie.

'Better get thinking,' said James.

'Always thought I would have years to get used to the idea of being a grandmother. Not so, it would seem. Can't decide how I feel about it tonight. Do know that I'm very, very drunk, though. How much further is it to the hotel?'

'Not far. Soon have you in bed, my lovely drunk wife.'

'Just don't expect a night of passion from me, will you?'

'We're grandparents. Why would I want to shag a granny?'

'Well thanks for that. Now I feel a whole lot better.'

Chapter Five – The Parry Family

The twins didn't believe in Father Christmas anymore. Grace had been gutted when, a couple of weeks earlier, they had sat her down, earnest expressions on their little faces, and Lily had said, 'Mummy, you do realise we know it's you, don't you?'

'But if you don't believe, he might not come,' Grace had said, trying not to sound too needy.

'We haven't believed for ages, actually, and we still got presents,' said Lily, folding her arms.

'We know about the tooth fairy, too,' said Jack. 'That was always Daddy. We used to try to stay awake, just to see.'

'But can't you just pretend? For a little bit longer? For me?' said Grace.

Grace knew she was wasting her time. Her children were growing up. Playground talk wouldn't allow them to believe, for any longer than was necessary, in all the childhood white lies that parents spun them. She was surprised at how disappointed she felt about it. Another milestone achieved in her little ones' lives. And could she really call them her little ones any more? In a couple of years' time they would mosts likely be taller than her.

Their Airbnb was only a short walk from the bar, but they had gone the long way home, walking back past the Savoy Hotel on Piazza della Repubblica, where they parted ways with the Hopper family, then looping back around via the shops on Via Pellicceria so that the children could see the displays in the windows. Some things about Christmas would always be magical, whatever age you were. Even if you didn't believe in *him* anymore.

'Don't they do it so elegantly here,' said Grace, watching the twins run over to a large department store window. A snow scene depicted all the usual things – polar bears, penguins et al – but in the middle of it stood a family of elegantly-attired mannequins, bedecked in designer ski wear and sunglasses. 'I know the London stores are as good as this, but round our way it's all the tacky old decs they've had for donkey's years.'

'Anyway,' said Tom, as the twins scooted ahead to the next window. 'What about that then, eh? Bit of a shock.'

'You can say that again,' said Grace. 'Poor Evie, I do feel for her. She was trying to make light of it, but you can see how worried she is, can't you?'

'And James just looked like he wanted to kill the guy. Poor Pascal will be lucky to make it out of this alive.'

'It doesn't have to be the end of the world, though,' said Grace. 'They'll get through it. It just means some adjustment, that's all. And Immy's a bright girl. She'll find a way to do well in those exams. Hopefully James and Evie will get their heads round it and see it's not all bad. We're all here for them, anyway. We'll do what we can.'

'People have to cope with a lot worse,' said Tom. 'Even so, I'm glad we've got a few years till our two give us those sorts of worries.'

'Yeah, me too. Wish they could stay like this forever.' They looked across at the twins, who stood in front of another window. Jack had flung his arm over his sister's shoulders and their heads touched, both sets of eyes wide with wonder.

'Whoever takes up with them will have to get past the other twin first,' said Grace. 'And that'll be a hard act to follow. I hope they're always as close as they are now.'

And then the moment was broken and there was Lily, running back to them. 'Jack pushed me,' she whined.

'Shh, you'll wake up all the people asleep in their beds,' said Tom.

Seeing that she wasn't going to get any sympathy from her parents for this latest minor spat, Lily stomped back to her brother, who stood there with open arms, waiting for her to come back to him.

'If you think I'm hugging you again after that, you've got another thing coming,' she said, folding her arms across her chest.

'What were you just saying?' laughed Tom.

'How about a nightcap on the balcony?' said Grace. They had finally settled the twins in their beds amid much excitement about bidets, strange chain pulls on the toilet and princessy curtains over her bed, as Lily called them.

'How did they know we were going to be a boy and a girl?' Lily had asked.

43

'Because we told them,' said Grace. 'They said they had special bedding, depending on what you were, and what age.'

'But how did they know I'd want to sleep in this particular bed?' said Lily. 'What if I'd wanted Jack's one instead? His is closer to the table where I've put all my stuff, so I might have done.'

'Well do you?' said Tom. 'I'm sure Jack would put up with pink drapes if he had to.'

'No I wouldn't,' said Jack, snuggling into his stereotypically blue bed and hanging tight onto the blankets. 'This one's mine.'

Grace kissed their heads and as the door clicked shut behind her, she knew they would be asleep almost instantly. It had been an exhausting and exciting day for a pair of ten-year-olds. For a pair of forty-somethings, too, she thought, yawning. She and Tom wouldn't be far behind them.

It had been a long time since they'd had an overseas trip. Since the holiday in the Dordogne with James and Evie, which had been a treat from James for Tom's fortieth, they had only managed a package tour to Mallorca, one Easter. Generally they holidayed in the UK, and it suited them fine. Sometimes it was easier with young children just to be able to load the car up and go, and provided there was a beach, some occasional sunshine, and a restaurant or two within walking distance, then their needs were few. For this holiday James had again made a very generous offer, to put them up at the Four Seasons with him and Evie, but Grace and Tom felt they couldn't accept – it was far too generous. Grace had nearly passed out when she'd seen on the hotel website that one night at the Four Seasons cost more than their entire stay in the apartment. They were happy here, within their means and with their independence.

The Airbnb had been a lucky find, just off the Piazza della Signoria. Given its central location, Grace couldn't believe that the price was correct until the kindly owner confirmed the booking, and then offered them many extras to help make their festive stay even more special. It wasn't luxurious, but it was warm and homely and they loved it.

Grace was so excited to be in Florence at last. She felt she already knew it, as Evie had sent her so many photos from her travels. As she stepped out onto the tiny balcony now, and craned her neck, she could just about see the statue of David in front of the Palazzo Vecchio, its spotlights making it appear bigger than it actually was. Grace thought back to the early days of her relationship with Tom, when Evie had sent her a photo of it with the cheeky caption 'He reminds me of your Tom, but only you can know how much!!' It made her laugh now to think of it.

'What are you looking so pleased about?' said Tom, joining her on the balcony with two glasses of Limoncello, one of the many welcome gifts from the owner.

'Oh, just feeling lucky,' said Grace. 'Happy to be here. With you and the monsters. We are lucky, aren't we?'

'We certainly are,' said Tom, leaning over to kiss his wife. 'This is going to be a wonderful holiday, whatever happens with our poor friends over the next couple of days.'

'I hope they're all going to be OK,' said Grace. 'Everyone's been looking forward to this for so long. I hope they can still have a lovely time, too.'

Christmas Eve dawned bright and sunny, but Grace and Tom's day had started when it was barely light, with a visit from two bouncy children who were keen to get the day started as soon as possible.

'So, Mummy, what's first on the agenda for today,' said Lily, straddling her mother on the bed, her little face serious.

Tom laughed. 'Have you got an agenda then, Lily?'

'No, not really, but I just want to make sure we fit in everything we all want to do.'

'What do you want to do, then?'

'Shopping,' said Lily.

'Oh, you are your mother's daughter,' said Tom.

'Of course I am,' said Lily, giving her father a puzzled expression.

'Go on that great big carousel in front of Bertie's hotel,' said Jack.

Bertie and Jack had begged to go on the ancient Pitti Carousel in the Piazza della Repubblica the night before, failing to understand why it was closed, just because it was late at night.

'Well, I'm sure there will be loads of time to fit in both. We've got lots of days to do things on. It's only tomorrow, Christmas Day, when everything's shut.

Mummy and Daddy really want to see the lovely art gallery, too. It's called the Uffizi,' said Tom, 'but we'll go there after Christmas.'

'Is that the one where Ana's Auntie Lydia works?' said Jack.

'Yes, that's it. Well remembered,' said Grace.

'I don't want to go there. It sounds really boring,' said Jack.

'It's not boring at all,' said Tom. 'The Uffizi is one of the most famous art galleries in the world.'

Jack's eyes glazed over. 'Can I go and play on my iPad? What's for breakfast?'

'Signora Rossi left us a lovely bag of pastries, so we'll have those. In a bit though, it's still too early.'

'So *can* I go and play on my iPad?'

'Go on, then,' said Tom.

Lily snuggled down between her parents for a rare moment of peace, away from her brother. 'I'm grown up enough to go to art galleries, but I don't think Jack is,' she said.

'You're both grown up enough,' said Grace. 'Sometimes when you go on a holiday you have to do things other people want to do as well. Jack will be fine. We'll find you both some interesting stuff to see. There are statues as well.'

'And a shop,' said Tom.

'Good. Are we going to see the others again later? What are our dining arrangements today?' said Lily.

Tom and Grace both shrieked with laughter.

'Well, we have a meal booked for this evening at the

hotel where Bertie is staying. And yes, with all the others. I hope that meets with madam's high expectations?' Tom prodded his daughter gently in the ribs, making her squeal with laughter.

'Yes, that's fine, thank you Daddy,' said Lily. 'Can we go to that bridge with the funny little shops on it, too? I saw a picture of it.'

'The Ponte Vecchio,' said Tom. 'Here we are, back to shops again. You really are a chip off the old block, aren't you?'

Grace had once been known as Queen of Shoppers, but that was all in the past. Before she met Tom, she and Mark had been together, and that lavish lifestyle belonged as much to her past as the relationship did. Things hadn't worked out for them, but she was as thankful now that Mark had moved on and found happiness with Alex as she was for the fact that the materialistic side to her personality was long since gone. Physical possessions weren't what made her happy anymore; her family was all she needed now. But none of that stopped her husband and friends from reminding her of the days when she had owned a walk-in wardrobe full of designer shoes, and shopping was her favourite pastime.

'Time to fire up the coffee machine, I think,' said Tom, pulling himself out of bed. 'If it's no good, then I'll need to pop out and find a café that's open at this ungodly hour. When will you two ever learn to sleep in?'

'When I'm a teenager, probably,' said Lily. 'Ana says you get to thirteen and then a button goes pop in your brain and you can't get up in the mornings.'

'Just don't grow up too quickly, though, you little monster,' said Grace, pulling her daughter close as Lily squealed with delight.

Chapter Six – The Hopper Family

Archie and Ana wanted to shake off the parents and have some time to themselves. Their relationship was still a secret; the two teens had always been great friends, but a few weeks before they had gone their separate ways on their travels, things had progressed to the next level. In a way Archie wished that they could keep it secret forever; he'd enjoyed the excitement of clandestine meetings and subterfuge, and with neither of them living at home, it was certainly easier.

'It's fine, thanks, Mum,' said Archie, when Alex suggested they all walk down to the Piazza together. 'Me and Ana are going to hang out for a bit. She wants to go to the Uffizi, I think, so I'll probably do that with her. I'm just gonna chill here for a bit first.'

Much as Alex would have loved to have her entire brood around her for the whole of the break, she knew it was unlikely that the older teens would want to spend all their time with their parents. 'I've missed you, love,' she said to her eldest, stroking his face. 'But that's fine. I'm just so glad you were able to come. You do what you want and we'll all meet for dinner later.'

'Thank you,' said Archie. 'Missed you too, by the way. It's good to be here.' He gave her a huge smile and her heart melted.

Archie didn't let on that Ana was actually going to do the Uffizi tour with her knowledgeable aunt – who was a senior curator there – first thing that morning, and in the afternoon the two of them had planned to hang out in a cosy café somewhere, hold hands and stare into each other's eyes. They had intended to tell everyone that they were an item on Christmas day, however now that Immy's news was likely to dominate the conversation, they weren't sure how well it would be received. Ordinarily they could see no reason why both sets of parents wouldn't be overjoyed that they were together – in fact they sometimes wondered why they'd decided to keep it a secret – but this latest development had made them slightly cautious about going public. It was bound to come out sometime, and they didn't want a big deal made of it, even though each was head over heels in love with the other and to them the relationship *was* a big deal.

Archie had been surprised and delighted when Ana had turned up at his ski resort unannounced, ten days before Christmas. 'Go out onto your balcony,' said the message which had pinged through to his phone one morning, as he was washing up after breakfast. He dumped the pans and ran outside to see a slight figure, with a holdall by each side, waving from below. Within seconds he was down there too, holding her in his arms, his heart pounding with joy.

'I've missed you so much,' he said. 'Why didn't you say

you were coming? I thought you were in LA for a bit longer yet. Didn't think I'd see you till Florence.'

'Nah, wanted to see a bit of snow. And you, obviously. Missed you.'

'Missed you, too.' Archie was over the moon. He held his girlfriend at arms length to study her properly. 'You look beautiful. You're so brown. And your hair. I love it.' Ana had swapped her long locks for a sharp bob whilst in California, and it suited her delicate features. They had FaceTimed and Snapchatted regularly, but nothing was as good as seeing it for real.

'Do you think you can cope with me here for a couple of days?' she said. She had secured a job at the resort, as a chamber maid at one of the large hotels. The job didn't start till after Christmas – she planned to head straight there from the Florence trip – but when her placement at a film studio in Los Angeles had come to a natural end she decided to go to Méribel early and see what the place was like, plus secure some good accommodation in advance of her start date. She had been offered a room in the hotel's staff accommodation, but had heard that they weren't great, and as she had saved some money, she wanted to find a flat-share, or a room to let with a local family, if she could. She still needed to go home before Christmas and collect the rest of her winter clothes and her ski gear, but she had two full days – and nights – to spend with Archie.

'Yeah, course I can. I can't quite believe you're here! I can show you the ropes. And the best places to ski,' said Archie. 'And my room. My bed is huge.' He pulled her close again. 'Come on, let's get you inside. My guests won't be back till lunchtime.'

'You're a bad boy, Arch,' Ana laughed, as Archie scooped up her bags.

'So, have you got somewhere to stay? Or am I smuggling you into my room for a couple of days?'

'No, you can't do that. I don't want you to get in trouble. I've booked into a hostel. Probably be a dive, but hey.'

'So, are we still going to tell them at Christmas?' said Archie. 'What do you think they'll say?'

The two nineteen-year-olds had grown up together. Grace, Evie and Alex and their husbands had been friends for years, and all nine children had been thrown into the melting pot at social gatherings for their entire lives. There was a friend for everyone amongst them: Immy was the eldest at twenty-one, and behind her Ana and Archie were the next down in age. The cluster of mid-teens had one another, plus they looked up to the older ones and babied the younger ones. No one ever felt left out when all three families were together; everyone just mucked in and got on with it, even as interests diverged, teenage hormones struck, and then again as little Lucie was added to the mix. For a four-year-old to have a raft of siblings and friends in their teens and twenties, plus twin friends the same age as Bertie, it was *awesome*, as she called it. There was never a dull moment.

As a result Archie and Ana had always been close as children, even though they'd gone to different schools. Now they were a couple, and crazy about each other, it felt as though this had always been inevitable. Archie was the first of the pair to realise that what he felt for Ana had matured from the cousin-like friendship they shared into something more intense, but he'd been worried to start with that Ana would find his advances creepy. It was only over the summer that he'd been brave enough to make his intentions known, and when he did he had been delighted to discover that she felt that way about him, too.

'I think they'll be stoked,' said Ana. 'Who wouldn't be, to have their two favourite kids hooking up?'

'Maybe we tell them tonight?' said Ana now. 'I bet Immy would love to have the attention off her for a bit.'

'No let's wait till tomorrow. Like we'd planned. One more day of our lovely, secret love affair,' said Archie, grabbing Ana's hand as they headed away from the Piazza.

Ana looked up at him. She couldn't wait to spend the whole of January and February in the same resort as him, before their year of travelling separated them again. They would have to get used to being apart, anyway. Archie was off to Plymouth the following September to take up his place on a marine biology course, and Ana was going to Bath to do psychology. The distance between the two universities wasn't insurmountable, but each was pragmatic enough to know that they needed to throw themselves into university life in their respective cities, or they would miss out on too much.

'So, show me the sights in this beautiful city, then, gorgeous,' said Archie, putting his arm around Ana's waist. 'Your auntie lives here, you must have been over loads.'

'No, not really,' said Ana. 'And when we did come, we

were just kids and we thought all the sights were boring. But Lydia showed us round the Uffizi this morning, and oh my God, it was amazing. She's got this way of telling you about art that makes you want to know more. She knows so much. It's really impressive.'

'Well it is her world, I suppose. I've never really got hooked by the whole art thing, but it's great that she can make people take interest like that. Maybe I should sign myself up for one of her tours.'

'Not before I've had you all to myself for a couple of days first,' said Ana. She pulled Archie to a halt in front of a street-side café and kissed him, before noticing that the terrace was just the cosy place they were looking for. 'This place has got patio heaters. It's perfect.' They squeezed onto a table in the corner of the packed terrace and beckoned to the waiter.

'We're not really getting each other all to ourselves, though, are we?' said Archie. 'I'm sharing a room with Bertie. I'd much rather it was with you.'

Ana laughed. 'Well, I'm on a sofa-bed at Lydia and Vincenzo's, so think yourself lucky. She's put Immy and Pascal in the guest room, which is right I suppose, though I can't think Mum and Dad would have been quite so accepting of it. Can you imagine Dad's face if Immy tried to share a bed with him at ours? Even though with the size of that bump it's quite clear my sister is no virgin.'

Archie laughed loudly. 'Oh, it's going to be so good to have you in Méribel with me. Seriously can't wait.'

The three families, minus the three eldest children, had

agreed to meet by the David statue in front of the Palazzo Vecchio at ten-thirty, and they would decide where to go first from there. As a party of twelve they were conscious of the fact that wherever they went, they were going to fill the place. They'd thought about splitting up, but the kids were loving their time with their friends, so they needed to make the big group work.

'Don't forget the carousel, Mummy,' squealed Bertie, jumping up and down. Lucie joined in with him, and then Lily and Jack, too.

'I think we'll need to bow to that pressure at some point, don't you?' said Grace to the other adults.

'First thing, or last thing as a bribe to be good?' said Tom.

'Let's do some culture first, then we can come back and do that at the end, if they behave themselves,' said Alex. 'I know for a fact that if our two have their treat now, they'll then whinge all the way around the museums.'

'Yeah, you're right,' said Mark. 'So, where to first?'

'How about the Duomo as it's the closest, then the girls want to do the Salvatore Ferragamo museum, then we could nip over the river to the Pitti Palace?' suggested Evie. 'And back here for the carousel later, if they've still got the energy.'

'Course they will,' laughed Tom, watching as the four younger ones climbed on the plinth of the statue.

'Sounds perfect,' said Grace. She and Tom had booked Lydia for a private – and more child-friendly – tour of the Uffizi on the day after Boxing Day, once all the others had gone home. As the only ones who hadn't been to

Florence before, they couldn't drag their friends round somewhere they'd already been – some of them many times. Alex wouldn't have minded going again, she said; she hadn't been to Florence since her travels with her first husband, Peter, but on a holiday like this, it was all about keeping the majority happy. Mark had visited on business just a few years earlier, and so he was happy to go with the flow as well. No one really minded what they did; it was all about spending the time together.

'So, before we leave here,' said Evie, pointing to the David statue, 'we need some photos with him. Especially you, Tom. I'm sure Grace has told you about my infamous text to her, when you two started dating.'

'Oh, yes,' groaned Tom, 'I've heard all about that. Many times.' He rolled his eyes as Evie steered him towards the statue. With his blond curls, now gently greying, strong jawline and broad shoulders, there was no doubting the similarity between the two, but his embarrassment was evident from the blush creeping up his face.

'Come on kids, off you get,' said Evie, shooing the little ones off the base of the statue. 'I'm sure you're not supposed to be on there, anyway.'

'Why's that statue got no clothes on?' said Lily. 'They should have carved him some pants.' The resulting laughter deflected the attention from Tom, for which he was glad.

'Want to see some more statues?' said James, steering the younger children away from David and his obvious attributes as Evie took her photos. 'Jack, you'll love some of these over here.' He led them over to the Loggia dei Lanzi, where Jack gazed up in awe at the wide arches and the statues beneath. 'This one's Perseus. Do you know who he was?'

'Yeah, he killed lots of monsters,' said Jack. 'Awesome. Is that why he's got a chopped-off head in his hands?'

'Really, James?' said Evie, coming over, and tucking her phone into her coat pocket. 'He's only ten, remember.'

'Yeah and ten-year-old boys love this kind of stuff,' said James. 'That's Medusa's head. She was the one who had snakes instead of hair.'

'That's so cool,' said Jack, his eyes wide.

'She's the one who turned everyone to stone in *Percy Jackson*,' said Bertie, taking a sudden interest.

'That's right,' said Mark, joining them. 'We loved those books, didn't we?' He ruffled his son's hair.

Evie smiled in amusement as she spied Millie and Rosie posing for selfies – which would undoubtedly end up on their social media feeds – in front of some of the other statues. Florence was so *instagrammable*, Evie thought, to coin a term her own daughters used a lot.

'Can we get ice-creams, Mummy?' said Lucie, bored with the statues already and skipping towards her mother. The delights of Florence – other than the vast array of ice-creams – were lost on a four-year-old.

'Ice-creams quickly now, then, for those who want them,' shouted James, clapping his hands and rounding up the children. Even the teens put their phones away. 'The best shop is over there, on the corner. Then it's off to the Duomo. Although you lot will need to wipe your messy little mitts before you go in there.'

Evie thought it was great to see him enjoying the company of small children again. She felt a sudden pang for the loss of her girls' childhoods, before it hit her with a jolt that the next young child in their lives would be their grandchild. In less than three months time.

'He'll make an amazing grandpa,' said Grace, reading her friend's mind as she caught up with her. She put her arm around Evie.

'Yeah, I was just thinking the exact same thing,' said Evie. 'Scary though, isn't it?'

'I think it's all rather wonderful, once you get used to the idea,' said Alex, coming up on her other side. 'We'll help, won't we Grace? We'll help Grannie Evie out with her grandparenting? I can't wait to have a cuddle.'

'What if I've forgotten what to do? Ana's nineteen, for goodness' sake. It's ages since I've changed a nappy.'

'It's like riding a bike,' said Alex. 'You never forget.'

'Yeah but you haven't had a chance to forget, with your lot,' laughed Evie. 'You've been breeding for years.'

'Thanks. I'm done now, though. With five kids between the ages of nineteen and four, I think I've done my bit for the survival of the species.'

'You certainly have,' said Grace.

'Oh, thank heavens for you two, what would I do without you?' said Evie, smiling at her friends. She linked her arms through theirs as they followed husbands and children to the ice-cream parlour.

Chapter Seven – The Tizzaro Family

Lydia had thoroughly enjoyed showing her nieces – and Pascal – around the Uffizi. They hadn't needed to queue for tickets as she could get them in on guest passes, but all the same they had started early to avoid the crowds. The gallery was expected to be just as busy on Christmas Eve as it was any other day, until it closed early, at three o'clock, so that the staff could return to their families in time for the evening's festivities. For Italians, Christmas Eve was a bigger deal than the twenty-fifth, but for once, Lydia and Vincenzo were foregoing their ritual Feast of the Seven Fishes with his family – Lydia was quietly relieved to have a break from it this year – and instead were joining Evie and James and their friends in town for a much more casual affair. This one wouldn't be seven courses; they all felt they needed to save themselves for the dining experience at the Four Seasons the following day. Plus the English little ones needed to get to bed in time for Father Christmas to come, whether they still believed in him or not. Her own children normally had their presents on Christmas Eve, as was the custom in Italy, and Lydia wasn't quite sure how she would explain to the English children that *Il Babbo Natale* came a day earlier here. If they put her on the spot she would need a ready answer.

As Lydia whisked them up the two steep flights of stairs into the entrance, Immy had to pause halfway for a rest.

'Sorry, it's tough carrying this ton weight around,' she said, holding onto a handrail to catch her breath and rubbing her swollen stomach. Pascal was immediately by her side, an arm around her waist to steady her, his brow furrowed with concern.

'No, I'm sorry, we should have gone up in the staff lift,' said Lydia. 'I do remember what it's like, being pregnant.' It hadn't been that long ago for Lydia; her youngest, Francesco, had just turned two. Immy had spent the previous evening, after they'd returned from the bistro, clucking over him, bouncing him on her knee, and delighting in his excited whoops of joy, even though it was well past his bedtime. Lydia thought she seemed genuinely excited about becoming a mother, despite her young age. She would be fine; her niece could handle this.

'Your mum and dad will come round, you know,' she'd said to Immy, as she watched Francesco pirouette around the living room, entertaining his grown-up cousins. 'It was just a shock for them, that's all. And I expect they're a little hurt that you didn't tell them about it sooner.'

'Yeah, I know. I realise that now,' said Immy. 'Would you have been upset if it was you? Do you think we did the wrong thing in waiting?'

'How you chose to handle it was entirely up to you, but I can see from your mum's point of view that it was probably very hurtful that you didn't tell them. Just go gentle on them for a while, give them a chance to come to terms with it, but don't worry, they'll soon get used to the idea, and then I bet you they'll be pleased as punch. Our generation is just a bit more conventional, that's all. I know accidents happen, but they probably thought they'd see you established in your career, and possibly married, although that's not such a big deal these days, before babies came along. It's just a lot for them to take in. But they love you so much and they'll be there for you. It will all be fine in the end.'

'I really hope so. I feel bad now for not telling them but I'm pretty sure they'd have wanted me to get rid of it, and there was no way we were doing that. We've loved this little blob from the moment we knew about him or her. And we were shocked at the time, don't get me wrong. We were taking precautions and everything, but it happened all the same. Finding out I was pregnant rocked our world, but because it did, we decided that, well, it was what life wanted for us at the moment, so we'd have to make it work. And we will.'

'So can we see the painting that your book is all about?' said Ana now, as they waited for Immy to get her breath back.

'Well, there have been a few books over the years,' said Lydia. As well as her semi-historical book, *Urban Venus*, Lydia had penned several titles. 'But I think I know the one you're interested in.'

'Yeah, the one where you had the dreams,' said Immy.

Lydia had spent a year in Florence as part of her art

degree, and it was here that she had met Vincenzo, who had been her tutor – and ultimately her saviour. She had been reluctant at first to share with her family quite how she had done her research for *Urban Venus*, believing they would worry about the state of mind of someone who kept falling asleep in front of the same painting – Titian's *Venus of Urbino* – and dreaming that she was the artist's muse, Maria. Over recent years – and once she knew for sure that her dreams were a thing of the past – she had begun to share her experiences with them. They had been shocked, but intrigued, to hear what she had gone through. Vincenzo, of course, had lived through the whole experience with her, and knew that it had almost cost her her life.

Lydia had never touted her book about Maria as a history book – because it couldn't be justified as one in the true sense – but nevertheless it had gone on to become a best-seller and made a name for her, though in historical fiction rather than art history. She had subsequently written some serious tomes, and they were the ones which graced the shelves in the bookshop at the Uffizi.

'Room twenty-eight,' said Lydia, leading her small party through the door. She loved coming in here, couldn't avoid it in her role as Senior Curator for Sixteenth Century Art.

'Is this the bench where you would sleep?' asked Pascal. He had only recently learnt of Lydia's experiences, and to begin with had found it hard to comprehend. 'Didn't anyone ever notice that you were there?'

'Yes, that's the one,' said Lydia. 'I don't think, Pascal,

that I was ever there for long enough. Although the dreams felt like they took ages, in reality I was probably only ever asleep for a few minutes at a time.'

'That's fascinating,' said Pascal.

'Why don't you three sit there while I talk you through what we have in here?' said Lydia.

Immy stroked the green leather of the bench distractedly as Lydia introduced them to the works of art: *Flora*, in her fresh-faced youthfulness, and the beautiful *Madonna of the Roses*. *Eleanora Gonzaga*, a formidable-looking woman, and *Francesco Maria della Rovere, Duke of Urbino*, her husband. And then of course, *Venus of Urbino*, which in Lydia's eyes was unsurpassable.

If asked by visitors who the artist's model was, Lydia had a spiel straight from the textbooks. But as she spoke, it would always sadden her that what she knew to be true about Maria was still unproven. Titian had been a world-renowned artist, but Maria was a low-class woman who had been plucked from a brothel, so it was unlikely that any record of her would have survived the years – if it had even existed at all.

As Lydia spoke, both young women and Pascal were transfixed. She had a way of making the knowledge so engaging. Immy hoped she could one day hold the attention of a classroom full of children like that, and that some of her aunt's talent for delivery had passed through the genes.

'Do you still feel drawn to the painting?' said Ana.

'Yes, to a certain degree,' said Lydia. 'I still find her really fascinating, but I've never had the urge to sit here again and submit to her like I used to.' Part of her was relieved, but a small part disappointed. It had been an incredible time of her life.

'I wonder what would have happened if you'd never come to Florence?' said Immy. 'She'd never have had the chance to tell her story, would she?'

'I'm a great believer in fate,' said Lydia, 'so I'd like to think I was always destined to come here and somehow she drew me in.'

Immy shivered. 'Are you cold, my love?' said Pascal.

'No, just makes you think, doesn't it? Fascinating, though.'

'So, do you think you and Vincenzo will have any more kids?' said Immy, as they sat on the terrazzo of the café in the gallery afterwards. It was over the top of the Loggia dei Lanzi, affording a stunning view across the Piazza della Signoria. The sun was shining but the air fresh, so they wrapped their coats tightly around them as they sipped at their coffees, watching the tourists beneath them.

'Immy, that's a bit personal,' snapped Ana. 'Just because you're having one, it doesn't give you the right to pry into people's private lives.'

'I'm sorry,' said Immy.

'That's OK,' said Lydia. 'I suppose you should never say never, but we've got our lovely little family now, one of each, so we're very lucky. And I love my job, so I wouldn't want to plan any more time out from that for the moment. They've both been easy babies, but I bet if we had a third, they'd be the one to keep us up all night.'

'Yeah, that's the bit I'm not looking forward to so much,' said Immy. 'That and boobs like melons.'

'I don't mind the melons,' said Pascal, laughing.

'Oh, don't look at me like that,' said Immy, joining in the laughter. 'I'm so not sexy at the moment with this great bump.'

'You are always sexy, my darling,' said Pascal.

'Hey, you two, we're still here, remember?' said Ana.

Chapter Eight – Everyone

The three ten-year-olds plus Lucie and Emilia were on their third go on the carousel. Immy and Pascal stood to the side, supervising them, whilst the parents sat on the outdoor terrace of the Bar Irene, in front of the Savoy hotel.

'I really can't wait to be a dad,' said Pascal. 'It's going to be awesome.' His near-impeccable English, delivered with a strong French accent, still made Immy swoon. She leaned over and kissed him on the cheek.

'Me too,' said Immy. 'A mum though.' They both laughed.

'We've got this, haven't we?' said Pascal. 'They might think we're too young, but we'll be OK. We'll be the best parents ever, won't we, bump?' He placed his hand tenderly on Immy's stomach. 'Hello Louis or Charlotte, whoever you are in there.'

'Charlotte, I reckon,' said Immy. 'I just have a feeling this is a girl.'

'I really don't mind what it is,' said Pascal. 'I just want it to be healthy. Oh, and the most beautiful child in the world, which it will be, of course. It has to be, with us as parents.'

Immy laughed, turning her attention back to the children on the ride. 'Look at them,' she said. 'Kids really are magical, aren't they?'

'Let's hope we're still saying that in a few months,' laughed Pascal.

'We will be, I'm sure. After finals, at least. Until then it's just going to be hard work and poopy nappies and I'm not underestimating that at all. We'll take it a day at a time.'

'We'll have lots of help,' said Pascal. 'Well, we know my parents are on side, and yours will be by then, I know they will.'

'I think Dad's coming round to the idea quicker than Mum,' said Immy. 'I've seen a funny look on his face when he looks at me. Funny good, not funny cross like he was at the start.'

'I think he still wants to kill me, though,' said Pascal. 'I think I will never be perfect enough for his wonderful daughter. And he is right, but I try to be as good as I can.'

'You are perfect to me in every way,' said Immy.

The Piazza della Repubblica looked spectacular, with festive lights everywhere. The terrace of the Savoy's bar still sported the huge umbrellas which shaded the clientele from the summer sun, but now was also dotted with patio heaters, tucked neatly in between. Thousands of tiny white lights were strewn around the umbrellas and across the entrance to the hotel. Grace thought she hadn't felt quite so Christmassy in years, as she kept one watchful eye in the direction of the children, and the other on the conversation with her friends.

'Aren't we all so lucky to be here,' she said, raising her glass. 'To friends and family, and thank you all for a wonderful Christmas.'

'And it's not over yet,' said James. 'The best is yet to come, tomorrow. Well, I hope so, anyway.' James and Evie knew that a Christmas meal at the Four Seasons would be a stretch on their friends' budgets, and so James had insisted on picking up the tab for all of the food, and then they would split the cost of the alcohol – which was still likely to be quite substantial – between the four couples. He wouldn't hear any arguments against it, pitching it as their Christmas present to their friends, and to his sister-in-law and her husband. None of them wanted – or needed – gifts at this point in their lives. What they all valued now was the opportunity to do wonderful things like this trip, and spend time with their friends and family. As the children grew up, and everyone's lives became busier, it had become increasingly difficult. The parents of the older children were so grateful that everyone had been able to find time out of their work, study or travelling schedules to be able to join them, but there was bound to come a time, in the not too distant future, when one or the other would be missing from the gathering. They had to cherish every moment.

The four fathers wandered over to the carousel, beers in hand.

'We'll take over if you like?' said Vincenzo to Immy. 'You two can go and have a drink.'

'Look at me, papa,' shouted Emilia as she twirled

around. 'I'm in a carriage.'

The other children had opted for the horses, which rose and fell gently as the carousel turned, but Emilia had chosen a carriage instead, holding her head high and shrieking with excitement.

'*Come una principessa,*' cooed Vincenzo, beaming at his daughter. Emilia was fully bilingual now, and it fascinated her parents how easily she flitted from one language to the other, even at the age of almost five, when many children were still trying to master their mother tongue.

'*Si, sono la principessa del mondo,*' yelled Emilia, proving his point entirely.

'It's so good to see you all, Vincenzo,' said James, putting an arm over his brother-in-law's shoulder. They had always got along really well. 'Evie and I have missed our little trips to Florence lately. She's just been too busy with her writing. Too many deadlines.'

'But she loves it though, doesn't she,' said Vincenzo. 'It's great that she has that, especially now the girls are grown and nearly gone.'

'Yeah, hard to believe they were once the size of these little ones,' said James. 'Everyone tells you they grow up quickly, but it's not until they do grow up that you realise how right they were. I've turned into one of those dads who says that to younger fathers now. You've still got years left, you two, so in a funny kind of way I'm quite looking forward to our grandchild coming along. It'll take us back to all that magic of childhood.'

'I thought you would come round to the idea,' said Tom. 'I think it's really exciting. Not what you'd planned for Immy right now, I know, but she'll make a go of it. And Pascal's a kind man with a bright future. She could do a lot worse.'

'Yeah, it's new beginnings, isn't it? You guys have your little ones still, and we're going to have a little one that we can borrow – and then hand back when we need to. I actually think it's going to be brilliant.'

'So Pascal's life is safe for now?' said Mark. 'No murder on the cards?'

'Only if he breaks my daughter's heart. Then I'll wring his little French neck.'

By the time Archie and Ana arrived, the women had already put in an order for a second round of cocktails.

'So where did you two get to?' said Alex, as the two teenagers pulled up chairs alongside them.

'Oh, just round and about,' said Archie, avoiding eye contact. 'Had a wander, coffee in that café over there actually, then a bit of browsing round the shops. Not much, you know how it is.' Ana smiled an awkward smile and kept her gaze downwards, too.

Alex and Evie exchanged a look, hoping their eyes didn't betray their suspicions.

'Do you think Ana and Archie are seeing each other?' Evie had said earlier that day, as they strolled around the Duomo, gazing up at Georgio Vasari's magnificent frescoes of *The Last Judgement*.

'Oh, I hadn't really thought about it,' said Alex. 'They've always been close, though, haven't they?'

'I've just noticed one or two looks between them. I

reckon something might be going on but they don't want to say anything yet,' said Evie.

'Aww, that would be sweet, though, wouldn't it?' said Alex. 'They make a lovely couple. They'll get my blessing, anyway.' Alex swung round to face her friend. 'Hey, that would be an amazing top table at their wedding, wouldn't it?'

'Let's not jump the gun,' laughed Evie. She clapped her hands to her cheeks. 'Oh my goodness, both of my girls in relationships. How will I ever cope?'

'They've grown up too fast,' said Alex.

'You can say that again,' said Evie. 'I wonder if they are planning to tell us at some point? It's quite cute that they want to keep it secret isn't it? I have to say, I did wonder when Ana announced that she was going to Méribel too. Oh, how exciting!'

'We'll just have to give them some space until they decide what they're going to do,' said Alex. 'Someone will catch them out at some point. One of the little ones, probably, and you know what kids are like, they'll just blurt it all out.'

'Poor things. It's lovely, though, isn't it?,' said Grace. 'I'm so happy for them. If your suspicions are right, anyway.'

'I'm pretty sure they are. You and I will be watching them like hawks now, won't we?' said Alex.

'We'll have to do it subtly,' said Evie.

'You're rubbish at subtle, Evie,' said Grace.

'Well thanks, friend,' said Evie and all three laughed.

'What are you lot laughing at over there?' said Mark,

coming over.

'Oh nothing. Just girly stuff,' said Alex, grinning at her friends. 'But we'd better be quiet, hadn't we? Don't want to get into trouble for laughing in church.'

The fathers allowed the children one more ride on the carousel before calling time on it.

Jack ran ahead, across the Piazza. 'I'm hungry, Mummy,' he announced, screeching to a halt beside Grace. The other children followed behind, skipping and running with delight – and so much energy for this time of the evening. And behind them, the fathers, deep in conversation. Grace was still relieved, even after all this time, that her ex-partner and her husband managed to get along so well. It was an unusual predicament for them all to be in, but somehow the friendships still worked, which was really important, given her enduring closeness to Alex.

'Well, that's good, because we're going in for dinner now,' said Grace, pulling him in for a fidgety cuddle.

It was pleasant enough under the patio heaters for aperitifs, but they had booked a large table inside Bar Irene for dinner. It was December, after all, and although they wouldn't have dreamt of sitting outside at home to eat or drink at this time of the year, there was something about the cold crispness of an Italian winter's day that made you want to be outside.

As they rose to head indoors, Grace noticed how Archie and Ana hung back.

'Don't look now,' said Grace to her friends, 'but I think your two lovebirds are waiting so they can sit together.'

'That's so cute,' said Evie. 'I'm hoping this is one relationship that James won't kick off about.'

'He's just a protective father,' said Alex. 'I'm sure Mark will be the same when our girls start dating. Whatever anyone says, it's that father-daughter thing, isn't it? No man is ever good enough for their girls. Although I'm sure he'll make an exception for my wonderful son, won't he Evie?'

'Let's hope so!' said Evie.

Inside, the eating area was only small, so their party of twenty took up the whole of one side. Grace and Tom were seated on a long bench at the back of the table, with a good view of the other diners.

'Uh-oh,' said Grace, turning to her husband and shielding her face with her hand.

'What's up?' said Tom, taking a large gulp of wine.

'Hide behind that wine glass, it's those women again. The ones from the car hire place, remember? Table to the left, over by the window.'

'Oh, God, how could I forget,' said Tom.

'What's that, Tom? You brought your fan club with you?' said James, too loudly.

'Shh,' said Grace, 'don't draw attention to us.'

'Yeah, like no one's going to notice us lot, with all the noise they're making down that end,' said Millie. She had decamped from the middle of the table firmly to the adults' end, declaring the children's end to be *like a zoo*. At seventeen, she didn't see why she needed to be with the kids; Rosie could keep the peace down there, plus she liked children more than Millie did. The fact that it was largely the Hopper children – her own siblings – making all the noise only convinced her further to move away. Lily, Jack and Emilia were far more tolerable, and little Francesco just sat on his mum's lap all the time anyway, almost asleep. She refused to sit with them, amidst a sea of bread stick crumbs and apple juice, when the alcohol and fancy canapés were at the adult end.

Grace had already regaled the friends with the story of the two women who had accosted Tom at the airport.

'So have you worked out who they thought you were?' said Evie.

'Haven't a clue,' said Tom. 'Maybe someone from one of the soaps. Or *I'm a Celeb*, or something like that. We don't watch half of the stuff that's on TV, so I expect we'll never know.'

'Oh shit, I think they've spotted you,' said Alex. 'And yes, they're coming over.'

'No way,' said James. 'You just wouldn't, would you?'

'If it was your TV idol, then maybe you would?' said Evie.

'I don't have any TV idols,' said James. 'Well, only Alesha Dixon, but I think I'd be too busy pulling my chin off the ground if she walked in.'

'Here we go. Brace yourselves everyone,' laughed Mark.

The two women walked across the bar, clearly on the pretence of going to the toilet, but then they stopped by the friends' table.

'Hello, again,' said the one who wasn't Shirley. 'Do you think we could trouble you for a selfie? We didn't like to ask when you were busy getting your car the other day.'

'Well, you could, but like I said, I'm really not who you think I am,' said Tom.

'He's so modest, isn't he?' said Shirley to Grace, clearly hoping that Grace would tell them he was always like this, and he just did it to fight off fans.

'He really isn't famous, you know,' said Grace, trying to be patient. 'Who is it that you think he is?'

The two women giggled and nudged one another. 'She's in on it too,' said one. 'Um, well, Bradley, obviously,' said the other.

'Bradley Walsh?' piped up James, slapping the table as he laughed at his own joke.

'Bradley Wiggins,' said Mark.

'Brad Pitt?' laughed Immy.

The two women looked deadly serious. 'Bradley Cooper,' said Shirley, as though it was the most obvious thing in the world, and they were all idiots for not realising they were out for dinner with a Hollywood superstar.

'Jeez,' said Ana, 'this is so embarrassing. This is just my dad's friend, and he's called Tom Parry and he's the headmaster of a private school in Worcester.'

'But clearly as handsome and charismatic as Bradley Cooper,' said James, his face now deadpan again.

'Obviously,' said Grace. 'Why do you think I married him?'

'You can have a selfie with me instead, if you like,' said James, jumping from his chair at the end of the table. 'I'm Chris Hemsworth. You'll know me as Thor.'

The adults collapsed into fits of giggles. 'James, you're

so naughty,' said Grace. And then to the two women: 'I'm so sorry, but you are actually quite mistaken. None of us is famous, I'm afraid. But it was lovely to meet you both, and I hope you have a wonderful Christmas.' She hoped that would dismiss them, once and for all.

As the two women moved away, Grace overhead one of them say: 'Oh well, still no selfie. He's so nice, though, isn't he? Just very shy. And he was so confident on Graham Norton the other week.'

'His hair looks a bit lighter in the flesh, doesn't it?' said the other. 'Didn't expect him to be quite so grey.'

'Well, that was a fun night, wasn't it Bradley,' said Grace, as Tom brought their customary Limoncellos onto the balcony.

'They still really did think I was him, didn't they?' he said. 'Nothing was going to convince them, was it?'

'I don't think you look anything like him, to be honest,' said Grace. 'You're far more handsome.'

'I love you too, gorgeous wife,' said Tom, kissing her.

'And your hair's all wrong.'

'They wouldn't have it though, would they?' said Tom. 'Hilarious.'

Grace laughed. 'I hope the kids can sleep after all the excitement.'

'Sure they'll still be out of bed at six, wondering if Father Christmas has managed to find his way to Italy.'

'Even though they don't believe. Still gutted about that,' said Grace.

As they gazed across at the spot-lit view, the church

bells began to chime midnight.

'Merry Christmas, my love,' said Grace.

'Merry Christmas to you too, my darling,' said Tom. 'We should get to bed. I don't expect this night to be very long.'

Chapter Nine – Christmas Day

'Ah, signore e signora Brookes, buon natale a voi!' Evie and James were the first ones to arrive in the Atrium bar, where they were greeted again by Ludo. Evie had to wonder how much time the poor staff ever had off.

She hadn't slept well: a combination of too much good food, cocktails and wine plus, despite the wonderful atmosphere of the evening and her daughter's generally high spirits, she was still worried about the impact that Immy keeping the pregnancy secret would have on their relationship in the long term. The baby was one thing – what was done was done, and they would get through it somehow – but she hoped to goodness she and Immy could get back to the closeness they once shared. She wondered if Immy realised just how upset she felt about being excluded.

She hadn't had a chance to speak to Immy alone the previous evening, but she hoped they would have the opportunity for a few moments together before they all left for home. Immy would be going back to Paris with Pascal until the spring term at Exeter started, sometime in mid-January, and speaking on the phone or via FaceTime just wasn't the same. She needed to know, before they all left in two days' time, that everything was OK between them.

'*Buon Natale anche a voi,*' said James, beaming at the bar tender, and disproportionately pleased with himself for his ability to reply in Italian. Evie was always slightly envious of how quickly James picked up languages. Despite their numerous trips to Florence – and other parts of Italy – over the years, Evie had never got much beyond mastering a few simple greetings, but James seemed to absorb new vocabulary like a sponge, and he could deliver it in a passable accent too.

'Two Atrium mojitos?' said Ludo, reverting to English.

James looked at Evie. 'Shall we start on those, and move onto the fizz when the others arrive?'

'Sounds good to me,' said Evie. She was determined to enjoy herself today, no matter what.

'New bracelet looks beautiful, by the way,' said James, taking his wife's hand and gently turning her wrist. The diamonds in the tennis bracelet he had presented her with that morning sparkled under the Christmas lights. It was extravagant, he knew that, but each day he still thanked his lucky stars that she had taken him back. Where would he be now, if she hadn't? After a moment of stupidity a few years ago, which had almost destroyed his business as well as his marriage, he had vowed that he would spend the rest of his life making it up to her. An alternative to the life they shared now was unthinkable.

They'd had a lazy morning, waking up late, languishing in their huge bed, then managed a short walk in the low

80

winter sun around the back streets of Florence. 'Come on, I need to make some space for all that food,' Evie had said, as she'd dragged a reluctant husband from the bed. 'We need to get out for a while.'

They had FaceTimed the girls at Lydia's to wish them a merry Christmas; their presents would have to wait for later. It wasn't the first year that they'd not seen their daughters on Christmas morning, and Evie was nostalgic for the days when they would both wake early and rush downstairs to see what Santa had brought. They were magical times and now all gone. But next year there would be a new little one in their lives. Christmas with a nine month old baby – that had to be something to look forward to, didn't it?

For the girls they had bought a simple but elegant piece of jewellery each, although if they'd known sooner about the baby, then they might well have chosen differently for Immy. With Pascal's job, it was a relief to know that money wasn't going to be an issue for the young couple, but there was just so much to buy when a baby was on the way. Evie loved shopping; perhaps Immy might pop home one weekend before the semester began and the two of them could go and choose baby clothes together. It could be a way to bring them closer again, couldn't it? She would suggest it to Immy later.

'Can't wait to see you, darlings,' she'd said to the girls. 'Drinks at two, remember.'

'Don't worry, Mum,' said Ana, 'we'll be there. Never turn down the opportunity to dine somewhere posh, you know us. Especially when Dad's paying!'

'Cheeky,' said Evie, laughing as she ended the call.

The next to arrive were the Tizzaros. As Evie and James rose to greet them, Evie couldn't help but swoon at little Emilia's beautiful velvet dress.

'Oh my goodness, you look like a princess,' said Evie, bending down to kiss her niece.

'If we keep telling her that, she's going to start believing it,' said Lydia.

James called Ludo over as Vincenzo regaled them with tales of their manic but magical Christmas morning, which had begun very early.

'The others slept in,' said Lydia. 'Lucky things. They'll be along shortly. Immy was having a bit of a wardrobe dilemma. The dress she brought for today is suddenly too tight, so I left Ana in charge with a needle and thread. Oh, and then Archie turned up to see Ana, so he'll be catching a cab in with them, too.'

'Oh, did he now,' said Evie in a knowing voice.

'Another romance blossoming?' said Vincenzo, scooping his small son up into his arms. They were like two peas in a pod, Evie thought, Francesco sharing his father's dark hair and deep brown eyes. He was a beautiful child.

'Yes, we think there might be,' said Evie. 'Well, me and the girls think so, anyway. Nothing's been said yet.'

'Oh how cute,' said Lydia.

The Hoppers were next – minus Archie. Alex looked stunning in a simple red dress, and as she walked in alongside Millie and Rosie, it was clear that as many eyes were on her as on her two slim and lovely teenage daughters in their thigh-skimming cocktail dresses. Mark quickly rushed to put a protective hand in the small of his wife's back.

Lucie, too, had a new dress, and she bounded up to Emilia so that the two girls could compare outfits and swish their netted skirts together. Bertie fidgeted with the collar of his shirt. He was pristine and tidy for the moment but Alex didn't expect that to last much beyond the first course.

Lily and Jack came bouncing into the bar ahead of their parents, both rosy cheeked with excitement and also dressed in their finest. Grace and Tom sauntered in behind them, their eyes betraying a late night followed by an early start.

'Champagne for everyone?' said Ludo, already opening the second bottle.

'Be rude not to,' said Evie, finishing her cocktail quickly. Their girls hadn't yet arrived, but Pascal had messaged to say they were in their taxi.

And then finally the full twenty were present. Immy looked wonderful, Evie thought, absolutely blooming, despite the dress looking a little tight around the middle.

'I had to sew her into it,' said Ana, rolling her eyes. 'She'd just better not leap about too much, or the whole thing could go pop.'

'So no dancing on the tables later then?' said Immy, a wicked smile teasing at the corners of her lips.

'Definitely not in here,' said James.

'Joking, Dad,' said Immy. She exchanged a knowing glance with her sister and Pascal.

No one – other than Evie and Alex, who were looking for signs – had noticed that Ana and Archie had walked into the bar holding hands. Evie thought it was probably just as well; it was bound to come out at some point, and then the poor couple would be swamped with attention.

'Wow,' sighed Alex, as they were ushered through into *Il Palagio*. In the Michelin-starred restaurant the marbled floor gleamed, chandeliers twinkled and the pristine white tablecloths sparkled with gleaming silver cutlery and polished glasses. Tiny silver and white decorations festooned the ceilings and walls, and on each table stood a crystal centrepiece.

'Will we get Christmas crackers, Mummy?' asked Lucie, looking up at her mother.

'I don't know sweetie,' said Alex. 'I've no idea if they have crackers over here, we'll have to wait and see, won't we.'

'Oh,' said Lucie, her bottom lip protruding. Alex was slightly nervous about bringing her two younger children to such a special restaurant, but James had assured her that things were different in Italy. Children in restaurants were celebrated, rather than frowned upon, he had said, though Alex couldn't imagine them celebrating Bertie and Lucie too much, if they decided to kick off at the wrong moment.

'Ah, signora,' said the Maitre d', whose name badge read Patrizio Cipriani. 'And the little darlings. A very merry

Christmas to you all.'

'And to you,' said Alex, wondering if he would be quite so welcoming once the children had had their first spill of the day.

'Do we have a seating plan?' said Lydia, as they crowded around the table.

'Anyone anywhere, I think,' said James. 'And then let's swap between courses as there are so many of us.' There were to be seven courses, most of them delicate little offerings, but they didn't expect to leave the table until well into the evening.

Grace had come armed with activities for her children to do, and she pulled a couple of colouring books from her bag to begin with. 'There is no need to worry, signora,' said another waiter as he pulled out a chair for Grace. 'The little ones, they fine to get down from the table and run around. This is Italy! We love children!' He waved his arms in the air, in true Italian style. Surveying the other diners, none of whom had such young children with them, Grace wasn't so sure how well that would go down. But dining somewhere like this was an amazing experience for them all – and not something she and Tom could do often – so she was determined to enjoy it, whether the kids were models of perfection or not. After a few glasses of wine she doubted she would worry quite as much.

The meal was a set menu, with some tweaks for those who didn't eat certain things. The tens-and-unders were to get their own special set menu, and Alex and Grace looked on in wonder as a spectacular arrangement of focaccia, grissini and olives arrived to start them off, and the little ones pounced on it as though they hadn't eaten in days. The adults and teens gasped as their own first course was brought out – *Timballo di granchio reale* – a perfectly tiny portion of king crab in a sauce. It was exquisite. The table was momentarily silenced in honour of the divine flavours.

'Oh my goodness, that's so good,' said Grace. 'Can we come again next year?'

Tom laughed. 'Only if we win the lottery.'

As they reshuffled the seating plan ready for the next course, Evie found herself next to Immy at last. Pascal was on Immy's other side, and whilst he was deep in conversation with Ana and Archie – who had managed to remain next to one other, too – Evie thought it would be a good chance for them to have a chat.

'So, how are you, darling?' said Evie.

'I'm good, Mum. Really good, actually. And I love these earrings, thank you so much.'

'If we'd known, then…'

Immy cut in. 'I know Mum, and I really wish now that we'd told you. We weren't trying to hurt you, or exclude you or anything, it just seemed like the right thing to do at the time.'

'But I thought you knew you could tell me anything. I've always told you I won't judge,' said Evie.

'I know, and I'm so sorry. I realise now that I've hurt you both. I didn't think that telling Pascal's parents and not you two would have such a big impact.'

'We love you, darling, and we'll do anything to help you, you do know that, don't you?'

'Of course I do,' said Immy. 'I just wish I could turn back the clock and do things differently now. And then I'd tell you, right from the start. Please don't be sad, Mum. I want you to be happy for us. Can you be happy?'

'There's an old expression,' said Evie, 'that you're only ever as happy as your least happy child. And it's so true. But I can see that Pascal and this baby make you happy, and everything else surrounding that is for me to deal with, not you. And I will. As long as it's genuinely what you want, darling, then we are happy for you, really we are.'

'I think Dad came round to this quicker than you, don't you?' said Immy. 'You should have seen him yesterday, playing with Francesco, and then he was looking at me all doe-eyed, like he couldn't wait. It's a step up from wanting to kill Pascal, I suppose?'

'Oh, I'm sure he'd still kill him if the need arose,' laughed Evie. 'That's your dad for you. Protective father through and through. Are *we* OK though? You and me, I mean? I can't bear the thought that something has come between us.'

'Nothing has come between us, Mum. I made a mistake not telling you and I understand that now. I really am sorry.'

'Don't be sorry, just be happy. Enjoy this special time.' Evie pulled her daughter close and stroked her hair, kissing the top of her head gently. 'Anyway, you and I need to go on a shopping trip before uni starts,' she said, taking a deep breath and pulling herself together. 'We have so much to buy. Cute baby clothes and all the mountains of kit you're going to need. Can you fit in a weekend at home at some point?'

'Too right I can. Wouldn't miss it for the world.'

'The wine waiter fancies you, Mum,' said Millie to Alex. All of the waiting staff were very attentive, but the sommelier, Vito, seemed to be paying particular attention to Alex's glass. Hers was always the first one to be filled. They had opted for wine pairings with the courses, and Alex was struggling to keep up, though that didn't stop the sommelier from making sure that she always had hers first. They had only reached the fourth course, *Branzino arrostito*, roasted seabass with parsnip velouté. It was exquisite, but Alex wasn't sure she could cope with a fourth glass of wine – albeit a small one – being lined up in front of her. She wasn't a big drinker at the best of times, but Vito seemed to have high expectations of her trying everything.

'Don't be daft, he's closer to your age than mine,' laughed Alex. She looked up at Vito, caught his eye and he blushed.

'Should I be jealous here?' said Mark, leaning across. 'Looks like I have a bit of competition. Although I think I might lose that one hands down. Those Mediterranean looks and all that. Don't go falling for the younger man, will you, and leaving me in the lurch with all these kids.'

'Don't be silly, love,' said Alex, laughing awkwardly. She knew Mark couldn't normally bear it if he thought someone was paying his wife too much attention, but he was taking this surprisingly well, she thought. It must be the alcohol.

Lily, Jack and Bertie came screeching back to the table,

bursting with excitement.

'Ana and Archie are kissing by the toilets,' shrieked Lily.

'And he had his hand on her bum,' said Bertie.

'Oh my God, that's gross,' said Rosie. 'That's almost incest. I mean, they grew up together. It's like kissing your brother. Yuk.'

'Oh dear, the secret's out,' said Evie.

'You mean you knew?' Millie rounded on her mother. 'How could you know this and not tell us? My own brother, in a relationship with one of our best friends, and you didn't think we needed to know? How could you keep a secret like that?'

'Calm down, darling,' said Alex. 'We didn't *know*, we just had an inkling. And in any case, they hadn't told anyone, so we had to respect their privacy. It's up to them, isn't it?'

'Well, if they're going to go around snogging in public places, it isn't much of a secret any more, is it?' said Rosie.

'What's not a secret?' said James, breaking off from an earnest discussion with Mark and Tom.

'Archie's got a girlfriend,' said Jack. 'And it's Ana.' He announced the last part with a flourish, waving his hands in the air.

'Bertie saw him squeeze her bum,' said Lily, folding her arms.

'Oh,' said James, his eyes widening. Evie watched like a hawk for the tell-tale signs that all was not well. 'Oh... well... really... that's... um... wonderful!' He turned back towards the other fathers: 'Hey guys, apparently there's another happy announcement.'

Evie noticed Mark blanch. 'No more babies, don't worry,' she said, putting her hand on his arm.

'It would seem our Ana and Archie have found love,' said James.

'No one said anything about love,' said Lily, 'just yukky wet kisses.' They all laughed.

'What do we do when they come back in?' said Grace. 'They'll know we all know now, won't they?'

'Mum knew before,' said Millie. 'And she didn't tell us.'

'Did you, love?' said James.

'Well, not so much *knew*, but we girls had our suspicions, didn't we?'

'Either way, I think it's quite lovely, actually,' said James. 'Even though you kept me out of the loop.'

'It was only really yesterday that we put two and two together,' said Alex.

'Phew,' said Evie. 'Looks like Archie's dodged a bullet there, then.' She caught the despondent look on Pascal's face and felt desperately sorry for him. He had always known that he wasn't who James would have chosen for his eldest daughter.

James noticed it too. 'I'm so sorry, Pascal,' he said. 'I know you and Immy will make a go of things, and I'm sorry for anything I might have said in the past to doubt you.'

'Wow,' said Evie, sitting back in her seat. 'Now I've heard it all.'

'Thank you, sir,' said Pascal. 'I really appreciate that.'

'So do I, Dad,' said Immy, reaching over to put a hand over her father's. 'Thank you.'

90

Bertie had already lost interest in his older brother's love life. 'When's the turkey coming?' he bellowed from the other end of the table.

'It won't be turkey today, sweetheart,' said Alex. 'They don't have turkey for Christmas dinner here, I told you that.'

'Oh, but I want turkey, too,' said Lucie her voice a whine. 'It's Christmas, you have to eat turkey at Christmas.'

'Such wise words from her great experience of four Christmases,' laughed Mark.

'Shh everyone, here come the lovebirds,' said Immy. 'Make like we weren't talking about them. Act normal. Hey, you two. Good trip to the toilets?'

'That was rubbish,' said Millie. 'You're useless at acting normal.'

'Very funny,' said Archie. 'We know you all know now, so there it is. I'm sure Bertie will have filled you in, won't you, dear brother?'

'I saw your tongue,' said Bertie. 'Yuk. I'm never doing that to a girl.'

They all laughed. 'Oh, you will one day,' said Archie, sitting down.

'Never,' said Bertie.

'Anyway, we all think it's great,' said Grace. 'We all think you make a wonderful couple, don't we?'

'Good, and now let's change the subject,' said Ana, blushing as she sat back down. 'Look, pudding's coming out.' She was relieved as all attention focussed on what was arriving on their table. '*Zuccotto Natalizio, mousse alla ricotta con sorbetto al mandarino,*' announced the waiter. 'Ricotta mousse with tangerine sorbet.'

'Sounds far nicer in Italian,' said Grace.

'Oh my goodness, this is exquisite,' said Tom, diving in. 'Tastes like Christmas.'

As the dessert dishes were cleared away, Vito approached their table. 'Children, come with me,' he said. 'Come and look out of the window.'

The six youngest ones jumped down, little Francesco holding Vito's hand. He led them to the French doors to the side of their table and pulled back the muslin drapes. It had long since gone dark, but in the hotel floodlights the falling snow glistened silver.

'Oh, wow,' said Lily. 'Snow!'

'No way,' shrieked Bertie. 'Can we go out in it?'

Vito glanced in the direction of the parents for permission, then opened the doors. The little ones ran outside, shrieking with joy.

'It's snow, it's snow, it's snow!' yelled Lily.

'Isn't it wonderful,' said Vito. 'Snow on Christmas day, just like in the story books.'

'Real live snow,' said Jack, twirling around and trying to bite the snowflakes as they fell.

'Are you OK?' said Vito to Lucie. The little girl stood silently, staring up at the sky.

'I don't know what to do,' said Lucie. 'I've never seen snow before.'

'Well, when there's a bit more you can build a snowman,' said Bertie to his little sister.

'But I'm cold,' said Lucie. Vito scooped her up into his arms.

The parents and teens slowly realised what was happening. One by one they left the table and walked out onto the terrace. Across the floodlit gardens, the snow was beginning to settle. Just a little, but enough to add the finishing touches to a spectacular Christmas scene. It perched on the heads of sculptures, iced the manicured box hedges, and sprinkled the lawns as though they had been dusted with icing sugar.

'Wow, it's magical,' said Alex, wrapping Lucie's coat around her shoulders and taking her from Vito. There was that deep stillness in the air which only ever came with a snowfall.

'It's just like magic, Mummy,' said Lucie, shivering. Alex thought she still looked a little scared, but this was a whole new experience for her daughter.

'What perfect timing,' said Mark. 'Snow on Christmas day.' He put his arm around them both.

'Yeah, we come somewhere warm – well, warmer than home,' said Alex, 'and we get snow. The perfect end to a perfect day.'

'Hey, Mum,' said Immy, coming alongside Evie. 'Isn't it fabulous?'

'It is, isn't it?' said Evie, pulling her daughter close. Immy rested her head on her mother's shoulder.

'I love you,' said Immy.

'Love you, too,' said Evie. 'And that bump of yours, whatever it turns out to be.'

'Someone new and little for us all to love,' said Immy.

'Certainly will be,' said James, coming up behind them. 'Got a kiss for this old grandpa then?' Immy popped a kiss on her father's cheek.

'Come over here, Pascal,' said Immy. He had been holding back from a family moment.

'Welcome to the family, Pascal,' said James. 'You're one of us now.'

'Thank you, Monsieur Brookes. Or maybe now I really should call you James.'

'Yes, you should.'

'Immy,' said Pascal. 'I've been wanting to ask you this for a while now, or maybe I should ask your father first, but... will you...'

'No, Pascal,' said Immy, putting her hand gently on his chest. 'You don't need to do this now. I don't need to marry you to know that I love you and you love me and we're having a baby and...'

'Shh, just give me a kiss then,' said Pascal. 'It was all I was going to ask you for, anyway.'

'No it wasn't,' said Immy, giggling. 'It really wasn't.' She grabbed him and pulled him close, blowing the snowflakes off his eyelashes as she kissed him.

Acknowledgements

It has been a delight to pick up with my much-loved characters again, and to write something festive, even though the majority of the work was done through a very warm and sunny April and May.

I realised, as I wrote the last few words, that I'm still not finished with these characters. I have lived with them for more than a decade, and have seen them develop, their children grow up and their lives take interesting twists and turns. My characters are one of the reasons my job as a writer is not a lonely one. So I can safely say that there will be follow-up story at some point...

I'd like to say thank you to Jono Apparicio-Davies for another beautiful cover, and my first readers, Ginny Getting and Laura Pelling, for their valued input and honest feedback. And Alli Neal, as ever you are a wonderful editor – your attention to detail is second to none. My fourteen-year-old daughter, Emilia, also read an early draft, so thank you, darling, for telling me 'it's actually really good'. The best praise a mother can get! Thank you also to the staff at the Four Seasons Hotel in Florence for making my stay so memorable – no one looks after their guests as well as you do!

Florence is my favourite city in the world, and as we sit here in lockdown, it was a joy to revisit it again through the eyes of my characters. It made me yearn even more, not just for Italy, but for travel in general. Although this book is set in 2020, I decided to keep it in a pandemic-free world, or it would have been a very different story, and not the one I wanted to write. Fingers crossed that, by the time you read this in the lead-up to Christmas, there will be a glimmer of hope that the real normal will at some point replace the 'new normal'.

Thank you for reading and stay safe.

Sara x

If you've enjoyed this Christmas story, please take a few moments to **leave a review** on Amazon.

Want to read more by Sara Downing?

Find out what ended Grace and Mark's relationship, and how she met Tom, in *Head Over Heels*

What did James do, which put his marriage and business on the line?
Read *Hand On Heart*
(Or snap up these two books together in the *Head Over Heels Box Set*)

Love all things Italian? Read Lydia's story in *Urban Venus*

Also by Sara Downing:
The Lost Boy
The White Angel
Stage Fright

saradowningwriter.co.uk

SaraDowningWriter

@sarawritesbooks